Praise for R.G. Alexander's *Twilight Guardian*

"TWILIGHT GUARDIAN is filled with tantalizing moments, intrigue, and fantasy. R.G. Alexander paints a vividly enchanting world of which I immediately found myself immersed in."

~ *Romance Junkies*

"I thoroughly enjoyed reading this story and can only hope there is more to come..."

~ *Literary Nymphs*

"If you haven't read a tale by Ms. Alexander than I do recommend that you take the plunge. Her work is imaginative and highly sexual and she never fails to write a page-turner."

~ *I Read Romance*

Look for these titles by

R.G. Alexander

Now Available:

Children of the Goddess Series

Regina in the Sun (Book 1)

Lux in Shadow (Book 2)

Twilight Guardian (Book 3)

Midnight Falls (Book 4)

Not in Kansas

Surrender Dorothy

Print Anthology

Three for Me?

Twilight Guardian

R.G. Alexander

A Samhain Publishing, Ltd. publication.

Samhain Publishing, Ltd.
577 Mulberry Street, Suite 1520
Macon, GA 31201
www.samhainpublishing.com

Twilight Guardian

Print ISBN: 978-1-60504-563-4
Digital ISBN: 978-1-60504-529-0

Editing by Bethany Morgan
Cover by Anne Cain

First Samhain Publishing, Ltd. electronic publication: May 2009
First Samhain Publishing, Ltd. print publication: March 2010

Dedication

To Cookie—Love is the reason.

Many thanks to my supportive family, all the divas, and my beloved smutketeers Eden Bradley, Lilli Feisty and Crystal Jordan. Also Anne Cain, whose artistry has brought my characters to life in ways even I could not imagine.

Finally, Beth. You are, without a doubt, the best editor and friend anyone could ask for. Thank you.

Chapter One

A cloak of purple and blue descended over the mountainside, blanketing the world in shadowy twilight. His people knew these shadows well. They'd lived in them for millennia, guarding the Trueblood Mediator and his clan from harm. Honoring a debt to those who'd saved them from wandering the Earth as ghosts. Alone.

It was here, in the 'tween time, where Kit found peace. It wouldn't last long, but while it did he savored it. It was the only time he allowed himself to dream of a different kind of life. Personal dreams that weren't about duty and honor, obedience and loss. Though since he'd seen both his charges happily matched and mated, those dreams had become decidedly less satisfying. And far too short.

He walked the perimeter of both Were and Unborn lands, smiling in approval at the stealthy stalking of the young Weres guarding their property lines. He'd helped train them at their Alpha, Arygon Dydarren's request. They were good warriors, but even with their keen senses they never knew Kit was there. And that was as it should be.

The sky began its fade to black, throwing the stars into bright, twinkling relief. As it did he watched while his recent bedroom companion took off for parts unknown.

Elizabeth. He could only hope she would be all right. This had been coming for weeks, so he hadn't been surprised when she'd told him she was leaving during the last moonrise. It was the why that had confused him.

Kit had been sure all that had happened would satisfy her. That forcing peace between Unborn and Trueblood, Vampire and Were was the reason she'd changed Regina and created most of her clan in the first place. But since Sylvain and Arygon had started unifying all the scattered packs of Were on the nearby Dydarren lands, Liz seemed haunted. Nothing he did could calm her.

The last straw had been when word came from the elder Truebloods that they were offering a seat on the Clan Trust to a representative from the Deva Clan. The times had definitely changed.

To say Liz was disturbed by the information was an understatement. "Nicolette can have 'em. The last thing I want to do for the next hundred years is deal with those pompous, pigheaded prigs. Aye, I've had enough of that, and *them*, to last me twelve lifetimes."

Kit recalled chuckling at her accent, knowing it only slipped out when she was upset. He'd folded his arms across his chest, watching her flit around the room like an agitated butterfly. "I'm sure she'll appreciate that. I don't get it, Lizzy. Isn't this what you wanted?"

"Is it what *you* want? To be a warrior without an enemy to battle? No more than a glorified doorman when you are capable of so much more?" She looked stricken by her own words, stepping closer to caress his calf apologetically. "I'm sorry."

She reached past where he was reclining on the bed to grab her husband's dagger from its perch and placed it in her travel bag, blowing the red curls away from her face with a frustrated sigh. "It's what Mal wanted. Now...now I don't know."

The tough as nails, leather clad vampire had suddenly looked...lost. He'd had sex with the firebrand more times than he could count during these last few months. As soon as he'd arrived, escorting Lux and his two Were lovers to the safety of Unborn land, he'd actively pursued her. Who could blame him? She was vibrant and beautiful and had no desire to settle down with any man. He'd known her nearly as long as he'd been assigned to the Sariels, known her when she was newly married, newly Unborn. But last night had been the first time he'd seen her so vulnerable.

At last he had understood what was wrong. She'd been living for this all these years, for someone *else's* vision. Without that guiding her, she was rudderless. And there had been nothing he could do to help her, nothing that would ease her heart.

Though she hadn't been his true *grathita*, his blood mate, Liz still loved her husband—the late, great Malcolm Abaddon. Even if he had wanted to, Kit couldn't compete with a long dead hero.

He sat on his favorite tree stump in view of the castle, watching the lights of Elizabeth's small, private jet disappear. She'd been right. He was a Sariel guard. A warrior. If these alliances proved successful, and he believed they would, his job would become ornamental at best. Hadn't it already during his time at Lago Maggiore? Perhaps that was why he'd grown dissatisfied.

He was getting soft. Master Elam, his uncle and the man who had trained him to be the Mediator's guard, had always said a warrior's greatest enemy was to have too much time on his hands.

As for Elizabeth, he prayed that the Mother would watch over her and lead her to her true path. If anyone deserved to find happiness, it was Liz. And that included finding a man who only thought of her when she was in his arms and not another redhead. One who, unfortunately, didn't even exist outside Kit's fertile imagination.

His angel. *Sarasvatti.* His own personal, perfect creation. He'd started dreaming about her around twenty years ago. She was a funny little hellion then. A child who would randomly appear in his dreams of blood and battle, demanding *he* protect *her* from the images wandering through his mind.

He'd dubbed her his guardian angel, because her presence took away the nightmares and replaced them with laughter and a child's acceptance of the unexplained. She was never intimidated by his size or abilities.

All too quickly she'd grown. Up and out in ways that were impossible for him to ignore. He was never sure why he'd dreamt of a fragile human female. Maybe it was a fatal flaw in his makeup, this constant predilection for impossible situations. And she was the most impossible of all.

Kit closed his eyes as his thoughts drifted in her direction. He reached out with his mind, trying to conjure her image.

She came out into the clearing, batting away the branches that snagged on her blue nightshirt. A football jersey, she'd called it. He'd seen it often over the years, watching in delight as it grew tighter across her abundant breasts. And though the lettering had faded and there were holes around the collar, she hadn't thrown it away. He could only be grateful. No lingerie could be more enticing. In Kit's opinion, it was sexy as hell.

"*Sarasvatti.* Angel. You have come."

Her fingers tugged her shirt as low as it would go, which was just beneath the skimpy lace shorts riding high on the smooth, pale curves of her ass. She rolled her eyes as if realizing the pointlessness of her labors. "I was in the neighborhood."

A sound of pure happiness escaped his lips. "Ah, I've missed you." He hadn't dreamt of her in months, not since he'd been with Liz. He'd thought about her more than he wanted to admit, even to himself. There was no honor in acknowledging how often he'd closed his eyes and saw *her* crying out his name in ecstasy, instead of the flesh and blood woman in his arms. He liked to think it was his sense of right and wrong that had ended these dreamtime sojourns, but he knew it was guilt. Guilt for being unfaithful, not to Liz, but to a figment of his imagination.

She looked away, toward the castle in the distance. "You've missed me? I guess she's gone then. Did the pretty Unborn dump you? Leave you for a shorter supernatural being? A munchkin or a leprechaun or something?" Though she tried to sound merely curious, he could hear the hurt in her voice.

Knowing he'd caused her pain made him ache. She was the light to his dark existence. Strange though it seemed, she made him real. Kit couldn't let her maintain her distance, even if it was only for show. He wanted her passion. Wanted her to burn the way he did each time she was near.

He reached out, lightning swift to catch the hem of her shirt, tearing it up the center and tumbling her onto his lap before he answered. "She's gone. There's no room for pretence here, my angel. Not between us. Be angry with me or forgive me my imperfections, but these dreams are far too short to waste on icy pleasantries."

Her features softened, lips quirking as she sifted her fingers through the shreds of her tattered shirt. "I should be angry. It doesn't do a lot for my self-confidence when my dream man has a torrid affair with another woman. I should make you suffer a little. But... I've missed you too."

Kit slid his fingers between her curvaceous thighs, easily rending the webbed lace that separated him from her heat. "Oh I've suffered, angel." His thumb circled her clit while his palm cupped her sex, already wet with excitement. He loved how responsive she'd always been to him, more than matching his need with her own.

He slid one thick finger inside her, feeling her muscles tighten around him, the gush of her arousal easing his way. He growled. "Believe me, I've suffered." She shifted on his lap, her fingers wrapping around his forearm, hips arching against his hand.

"Yes. Show me how you need me. How badly you want it." She bit her lip at his words, her body writhing on his lap as he added another long finger, stretching her tight pussy with his thrusts.

Goddess, she was amazing. From the fiery curtain of hair falling down her back to her curling toes, she was the most sensual creature he'd ever seen.

His cock was iron hard and pulsing against her ass, demanding release. A release he knew he could never allow himself. Not even in his dreams. But that didn't stop him from fueling *her* desire. "Do you feel how much I want you, angel? How much I want to bend you over and fill you full of me?"

She whimpered, her free hand reaching up to pinch and twist her bare nipple. "Oh, I haven't forgotten those. I want them too. In my mouth, in my hands, pressed against me as I fuck them. Every wicked thing you've ever imagined is everything I want to do to you."

"*Yes*. Kit, yes!" She shuddered against him, crying out his name over and over while she climaxed on his hand.

He bit the inside of his cheek, tasting the blood that filled his mouth as he resisted his primal urges. He was satisfied with this. Just being near her. His angel. His test. He couldn't have more. But he could have this. He could give her pleasure.

Kit bent his head to kiss her damp forehead. "Don't you dare relax, *sarasvatti*. I'm nowhere near through with you yet." She half chuckled, half sobbed before turning in his arms to kiss him. She slid around in his lap until her legs were wrapped as far as they could go around his waist, fingers sliding through his long hair to pull his face down.

The greedy little temptress was driving him wild. Her tongue battled with his and he cupped the cheeks of her ass, as much to hold her hips still as anything else. If she kept rubbing against him like this he wouldn't be able to hold back.

"Angel, please."

She lifted her mouth and looked him in the eyes, her pupils so dilated he could hardly see the misty green for the black. "No. You made love to *her*. Really made love, not this constant foreplay." She bit his chin and laughed breathlessly. "I can't believe I'm complaining about continuous orgasms. But I want more."

He pushed her hair behind her ear, caressing her cheek, his hand trembling with restraint. "I've never made love with anyone but you, angel. The rest is just fucking."

"Then that's what I want. I want you to fuc—"

"Kit! Kit!"

Kit blinked, coming out of his daydream with a soft curse. He took a deep breath, camouflaging the scent of his need so as not to disturb the young Unborn jogging toward him. Hannah. He quickly masked his frustration with a smile. It wasn't her fault she'd interrupted his fantasy. In fact, he should probably thank her. Not that he would.

"There you are. Oh, Kit, Liz is—"

"Gone? I know. She left with the setting sun."

Hannah stopped in surprise, the note he'd watched Liz write the night before clutched in her hand. "You knew? I thought you and she were...*together.* Don't you want to chase after her? Stop her?"

Kit unfolded his large frame to stand, looking down at the small Unborn with an expression of good humor. Her eyes grew wide as her head tilted back to meet his gaze. Even after all this time, they were still intimidated by his size. But there was nothing he could do about it. Seven foot two inches was the limit he could shift down to in order to fit in with the smaller species.

"When you meet the person who can stop Liz from doing whatever the hell she pleases, be sure and let me know." He laid his hand on his chest with a sigh. "Alas, as dramatic and romantic as your plan sounds, I am not that man."

Hannah's blonde bob curved around her adorable pixie face as she studied him. "You don't seem too upset about it."

Kit shrugged. "Liz and I enjoy each other's company. She is an amazingly sensual woman, after all. But when you live as long as we do, you learn that there is only one constant. Things change. *That* is the secret of life. You either change with it or let it roll over you."

He made a face at his philosophical tone, causing Hannah to chuckle. "I sound like Priestess Magriel, don't I? Maybe I'm becoming a wise sage in my dotage."

The one-hundred-and-six-year-old Unborn, who still looked like a flapper from some nineteen twenties silent movie, had no idea what old was. Kit did. But his age wasn't something he shared with anyone.

Hannah shook her head, a relieved smile gracing her face, turning when one of the members of her clan called her to the house. She looked back at him as if wondering about the true state of his heart, before heading up the hill toward the sprawling castle that held Liz's ragtag group of Unborns, the Devas.

Their clan had had a rough road. He'd never believed that those Vampires who were "made", the Unborns, should be punished because the natural born Truebloods couldn't control their more unsavory urges. Until recently though, he'd thought his view was in the minority.

He was proud that it was the Sariel Clan, his charge Zander Sariel in particular, who had led the others in changing the archaic rules that demanded Unborn destruction and refused them protection from the Weres. Of course, they owed that miracle to Regina, Zander's mate, and previous member of the Deva Clan herself.

She'd changed everything.

"Did I hear that right? Liz is gone? Is that why you were drooling all over Hannah? Even a Were mid-mating season would wait a few hours before sniffing out a new conquest."

Speaking of Weres... "Jasyn Dydarren, fancy meeting you here. For a pup who hates Vampires, you spend a lot of time on the wrong side of their property line. Had a change of heart?"

The dark haired Beta flushed, looking away guiltily. "Don't be an idiot. My people *do* have a treaty with them now. And one of my brother's mates happens to be related to the Trueblood Mediator. It's not as if I can avoid them. I *am* ever loyal to my Alpha."

"Of course you are. Makes for a hell of a family gathering though." Kit chuckled. "But you'll excuse me if I don't believe you come here to further friendship between the species. At least, not the entire species. Just. One."

He glanced toward the castle, watching as Hannah ducked behind a curtain. He shook his head. "When are you going to swallow that fur-covered pride of yours and talk to her? Thinking of waiting another eighty years?"

Jasyn growled in warning, slamming a waiting Kit against the nearest tree. Kit allowed it, not making a single move to defend himself. He knew the pup was just releasing a little frustration.

Having the woman you loved turned into a vampire before you had the chance to mate with her was, as a Were, a fate worse than death. Besides, the boy didn't know what a Sariel guard could do. "Feel better?"

"It's none of your business. *She* is none of your business." Jasyn threw his hands out to his sides, stepping away as if he'd just realized what he had done. "Nor is she any of mine. She's just another bloodsucker with that French whore's blood running through her veins. The Hannah I knew died a long time ago."

Jasyn refused to look toward the window, though Kit could tell it took most of his restraint. "You're right. It's none of my business. I apologize if I overstepped my bounds."

The Were sent a disbelieving look Kit's way. "What bounds? From what my brother tells me there is nothing you can't or won't do. Walk on water, kill the pack leader of the Shadow Wolves...Why should you stop at meddling in other people's relationships?"

Kit faked an offended expression. Inside, he was glad none of his people had heard that. Sariel guards were trained to be unobtrusive. Invisible. "Meddle? A Sariel guard doesn't meddle. We plot. We scheme in secret silence. But meddle?" He shuddered. "Don't go repeating that, especially not to Arygon. He'd never let me hear the end of it."

Jasyn laughed. "You can take it up with him when you see him. He's the one who sent me to find you. *That's* the reason I'm here. One of your brethren has arrived on our land. And he's asking for you."

An icy feeling of dread coated Kit's body, despite the warmth of the evening. There were only a handful of reasons a Sariel guard would leave his post. None of them good. The sudden sense of loss was profound, and he knew. Everything was about to change yet again. Only this time, taking his own advice would be the challenge.

Kit's demeanor changed in an instant. He stood straighter, his height off-putting. The alert onyx eyes and stone-faced expression of the Sariel guard replaced the good-humored man Jasyn had known these last few months. The wary Beta's shoulders dropped, and he stepped back in instinctive subservience.

Here stood the guardian of legend, a beast to steer clear of. The one Sylvain, his brother's female mate and his people's *Antara*, had told him about. But Kit always seemed so laid back, so jovial. Jasyn hadn't really believed even though he'd known it was Kit who had slain Sylvain's father, Gyvain, pack leader of *Les Loups De L'Ombre*, the Shadow Wolves.

Jasyn owed the guard his life for that alone. Gyvain had almost killed Arygon and both his mates before he was felled. Though he'd never understood his brother's life choices, Jasyn knew Arygon's loss would have destroyed him completely.

Kit strode through the woods leading to the pack lands, but Jasyn couldn't resist the urge to glance toward the castle windows before he followed. "Great Mother."

This was torture. Eight decades had passed yet the pain was still fresh. And now, with Arygon as Alpha of all the Weres, Jasyn had no choice but to stand beside his brother in this new world. A world of supposed peace. But there could be no peace for him. Not with Hannah so close.

He could scent her in the air around him. Scent the truth that had chased him away all those years ago. Even though Nicolette, his father's illicit mistake, had transformed her into a Vampire... Hannah smelled like his. His mate.

The longer he stayed, the harder it was to pretend his anger outweighed his desire to make her his in truth.

"Almost. Almost got it. Just move a little...*there*! Gotcha. A bit more than I wanted to see but..."

Not a bad day's work for a glorified Peeping Tom. She chuckled wryly to herself as she slinked down the damp embankment where her camera bag lay waiting in the dark. Jesse's phone started ringing and she swore, reaching quickly into her jeans pocket to stop the noise. "Damn it."

"Hello to you too. Have I interrupted your art? A nature study perhaps."

"In all its nude and frolicking glory," Jesse whispered with a smile. "And you almost ruined their night *and* blew my cover. What's up, Adrian?"

"When are you going to stop working for that private dick and use your talent for good instead of evil? Or am I *not* talking to the award winning photographer who's had her pictures gracing the covers of National Geographic?"

Jesse sighed. "This is my last job for him. A favor, really, since I was the closest photographer he had. Apparently his nephew's fiancé isn't the innocent noblewoman he'd been led to believe. I gotta tell ya, this job isn't really doing a lot for my belief in true love."

Truer words had never been spoken. If she'd ever had any illusions about the sanctity of love and marriage, these last few months working for Rudy Vittori's detective agency would have destroyed every last one.

Adrien snorted. "You've covered war, flood and famine, and it's a little extracurricular *boom-boom* that's made you cynical? Leave it to you. Anyway, if you're through doing Rudy's dirty work, does that mean you're coming to visit soon? Your sister-in-law misses you desperately."

"Boom-boom? No wonder she misses me. Between you and the kids, she needs some adult conversation." Jesse laughed as she folded herself into her tiny rental car, holding the phone in the crook of her neck so her hands were free. "I'm sorry, bro, no can do. I have some...personal business I have to take care of."

Her tone must have revealed a little of the uncertainty she was feeling. She could sense his worry over the phone. "Sis, are you...wait a minute. Did you say noblewoman? Where the hell are you, jolly old England or something?"

"Actually, I am."

"Long way to go for a few dirty pictures. Are you okay?"

"I don't know. That's what I'm here to find out." She pulled out from behind the tree where she'd hidden the evidence of her arrival. "Don't worry, Adrien, I'll be fine. And I'll come back with some amazing shots for your scrapbook. Norwich is lovely this time of year."

"Okay, okay, I'm not even going to ask. Just be safe, little sister. And if Meredith calls you later, don't tell her where you are. She's likely to join you and leave me alone with no food or clean underwear."

"Stop, please. I can't take any more romance. Your wife is such a lucky woman." Jesse smiled softly at her brother's guffaw. "I love you, little brother. I'll be in touch." She tossed her phone on the passenger seat and tried to concentrate on the road.

This was insane. She should call him back and tell him she was on her way to the airport. There was no reason on Earth for her to be in England. Hadn't she just immortalized on film example number two thousand and twenty-three why believing in daydreams and fairytales was a heartache waiting to happen?

Yet that was exactly what she was going to do after she downloaded this latest proof of infidelity onto her laptop. Chase after a dream. She'd traveled across the ocean on a whim, a feeling.

He needed her.

Him. The mysterious man she'd been dreaming of most of her life. Not even a man—a literally larger than life anti-hero straight out of a story from the Brothers Grimm. The sinfully sexy, longhaired giant who lived a life of duty and honor, in a world full of creatures that Jesse could never in a million years believe were real. But he...he *had* to be. And for the last few weeks she couldn't shake the feeling that something was wrong. That their time together was running short.

Maybe that's why she'd been desperate to be with him last night. Though once again, before she could convince him to take her the way she'd been longing for, he'd disappeared and she'd woken wanting. She shifted in her seat, uncomfortable with the memories of her begging him to fuck her.

She never knew why he hesitated. They'd done everything else over the years. And she did mean everything. But he was never willing to take her all the way. The voice of reason in her head told her it made sense. If she'd never been with a man in her waking hours, she had nothing to draw on, no information with which to fill in the blanks. But that would mean he was just a dream. A dream that reached for her every evening when the sun disappeared, and the moon began to rise.

Magic time, her mother used to call it. Jesse could remember her dancing around the kitchen, singing her favorite song by The Platters. She would pull Jesse and Adrien around the room with her, spinning them around while they laughed at their wonderfully crazy mother.

They had danced until they fell into their chairs, and she would tell them how she'd met their father. How he'd appeared out of the shadows, out of the purple mist. He was big and tall, just like them, she said. And oh, how very much they had loved each other. Jesse and her brother believed every word until they were old enough to understand the truth.

Their father had abandoned them. He'd left their mother alone to take care of two rapidly growing children and a mortgage that forced her to work her fingers to the bone to keep food on the table. Left her to suffer through a long, drawn-out battle with cancer before she finally slipped away, believing right to the end that he would return.

And this man from her dreams, the one who seemed so real she could almost reach out and touch him, was just another fantasy. One that aroused her more than any flesh and blood man she'd ever met, but a fantasy nonetheless. Her heart's way of keeping her reaching for the moon, unable to have real relationships, a real life.

None of this logic changed the fact that she'd hopped the pond to England on the redeye a few days ago. Or that she was about to start searching for some pub that probably didn't exist, and a group of people she could only *hope* didn't exist.

And him. Kit.

Jesse turned on the radio, desperate for a distraction, and had to laugh. "Of course. That makes perfect sense." The last strains of that familiar song "Twilight Time" echoed through her car. An image of her mother staring hopefully out the window popped into her head, and her hands tightened on the wheel.

That would not be her. Maybe when she proved once and for all that Kit was just a part of her imagination, she could get on with her life. No more hiding behind her camera. No more regrets. It was time to wake up.

Chapter Two

Max had been the one to come for him. His cousin and fellow guardian had told him that the Old Ones had called Kit back to their people's settlement, a stone's throw from the Mediator's clan. Max would replace him in guarding Lux and both his *grathitas*—the *Antara* Sylvain, and Arygon, new Alpha of the Weres.

When Kit asked who the elders had chosen to take care of Zander Sariel, his wife and their young son, Max had given him an answer he still could not believe. Kaine. What were the Old Ones thinking, giving the most prestigious, most critical duty to the least qualified among them?

His mother had to have been behind this. She was good at twisting rulings in her favor. The old crone had always favored Kaine above everything—Kit, common sense, even her own husband. She'd coddled and spoiled him, granting him amnesty from the warrior's training that every other able-bodied male of his species entered as soon as they could hold a weapon. And that decision had its consequences.

His younger brother was a walking morality tale. He represented everything that was wrong with their people—sloth, gluttony and a tendency toward violence. Kaine guarding the Mediator was untenable, but Kit knew of no way to solve that situation except one.

His mother would have known how he would react. In fact, she was no doubt counting on it.

After Max had delivered his message, they took off immediately for Haven. On the journey, Kit became more and more certain that this was the reason he'd been summoned. What the Truebloods would call *mahan calati*. A mission that none of his kind ever returned from. The same one his father had undertaken hundreds of years before.

"I may just kill Liz for taking the plane the next time I see her." Nicolette hadn't appreciated the ground route they'd taken to arrive in Norwich. Unlike Elizabeth, the Madame didn't like to use her abilities unless absolutely necessary, which had made it a more difficult trek.

Traveling with her for her first Trust meeting, as well as the others who'd just decided, on an impulse, to come along, had been rough on Kit. Sylvain and Lux had actually left Arygon behind to "visit" Zander and Regina.

Kit could hardly believe Slyvain had been allowed to come when she was so far along in her pregnancy. But she'd been adamant. Lux had confided that between her abilities and her unpredictable hormones, neither of her mates were inclined to deny her anything.

And Jasyn. Well, he wasn't sure why Jasyn had tagged along, other than the mumbled excuse of a peace offering from the Were Alpha to the Truebloods and his desire to get away from the temptation of one particular Unborn.

They'd all noticed the difference in Kit's behavior right away. He couldn't stop the regret that pierced him at the hurt in their eyes at his renewed distance, but there was nothing for it. He was what he was. Not Trueblood, not Were, certainly not human. Just a Sariel guard who did as he was told.

He'd forgotten for a time. Become their friend instead of their silent watcher. They'd let him into their lives, their inner circle, and he would never forget it. In many ways the younger Sariels and their mates were more family to him than his own. But that, too, had to end.

When they reached Ye Olde Haven Pub, Kit communicated to Max in silence. He would scout the perimeter while his cousin remained behind to greet the Mediator and, more importantly, Kit's younger brother. He wasn't ready to face Kaine in his current state of mind. Hell, he hadn't seen him in forty or fifty years. He would have preferred to continue that trend indefinitely.

It was spring, the night clear and bright with cold. He'd grown to love this countryside, this cold, grey island and its charms. Kit grimaced. He needed to stop wallowing in melancholy. Perhaps in his next incarnation the Mother would grant him a chance at a life of his own.

"Do you know them?"

The whispered question made him smile, though he instinctively touched his sword and scanned the darkness. "Tell me you aren't alone, Miss Regina. The Mediator won't be happy when he realizes you're out without an escort. You still have enemies."

The dusky beauty made a face, and Kit had to swallow a smile. "I keep telling you to call me Reggie. Besides,—" her expression grew somber, "—Zander knew I'd be with you."

She lifted her chin toward the window facing the alley. "Lux told me you'd be here. Do you know this family?" Kit hadn't realized he'd come here again. Come to stand in front of the window of a small loft above the local sweet shop, the loft that had held the owner's family and his children for several generations.

The youngest grandson had married and taken over the business. They'd had triplets, three cherubic girls with full cheeks and constant smiles. Even crowded into that tiny apartment, they all seemed so...happy.

"They haven't invited me over for tea if that's what you're asking. But I check in on them from time to time."

"Oh."

Kit looked down at Regina, his eyebrow raised. "Oh? Just oh?"

She shrugged. "Yes, *oh.* I get it, Kit. I used to walk the streets of the village near Deva Castle whenever I could, to be a part of humanity again. To watch them fighting, washing their dishes, reading their mail. Most never having a clue about the dangers right outside their door. I was jealous."

Her insight stole his breath. She understood. He should have known she would. Not only a Reader, but one who used to be human. Of course she would realize what he'd never been able to share with anyone.

For all their mortality, there was something inherently special about humanity. He'd always seen it. Weak? Yes. Violent? There was no creature on Earth or in heaven that didn't have that capacity. But they were also ingenious, adaptable, creative in a way that continuously drew his admiration. They were beings capable of accomplishing much during their short, simple lives. Surviving against all possible odds.

The Great Mother certainly seemed to agree. Look at all she had done to protect them. She'd created the Vampire and Were species to guide and guard them, taught a special few how to destroy the guardians who'd, predictably, forgotten their place. Humans were a fragile but blessed creation of the Goddess. A creation he shouldn't be thinking about. And he damn well shouldn't be fantasizing about one in particular, real or not.

Because they were also the reason his people were nearly extinct.

"I should take you back."

Regina laid her hand on his arm. "Kit, wait. I wanted to tell you..." She looked away guiltily. "You know the priestess has been guiding Sylvain and I in our dreamwalking. We know that you're leaving for a reason that, though clouded from us, feels dangerous. So dangerous that Zander sent a message to your Old Ones, requesting information when Kaine arrived, but they refused. They told him the debt they owed was protection. That this was a private matter that didn't concern the Sariels. I've never seen Zander so upset. We all are."

She glared like a small, golden-eyed tiger. "And that Kaine fellow isn't a very good replacement for you and Max. You know, I actually caught him raiding the pub's liquor stores? I had no idea one person could drink so much."

Kit tensed and she misunderstood, rushing to apologize. "Not that I mind. You've just always been so disciplined that I didn't expect it. And that's beside the point. I just wanted you to know that if there is anything we—"

"Reggie." Kit took a breath, finding his usual mask of serenity difficult to hang on to. "I appreciate it. I really do. You've all done more for me than you'll ever know. More than I've deserved. I am forbidden to tell you what you want to know, but I can give you my word, you'll not be under Kaine's protection for long. And the sooner I leave, the sooner I can make good on that promise."

"Mama? Mama!"

"In the name of the Mother!" Kit clenched his jaw until it ached. He refused to believe that Kaine was his blood kin. He scooped a surprised Regina in one arm and the giggling toddler who'd just wandered alone into the alley in the other. He'd have a word with Max too. His brother shouldn't be left alone with a houseplant, let alone the future Mediator of the Clan Trust.

As angry as he was, the image that greeted him when he slipped in through the back door into the kitchen of the pub was too comical to resist. His lips twitched as seven heads turned toward the door, jaws dropping simultaneously at the sight of the giant guardian and his two flailing passengers.

He took the scene in within moments. They must have realized the child had disappeared. Zander and Max had Kaine pressed against the stove. Nicolette, Jasyn and Lux stood protectively in front of Sylvain, who looked as if she wanted in on the action, pregnant belly or not.

Kaine had no idea the ethereal female was the most dangerous creature in the room. Apart from the one Kit was currently dangling from his biceps.

"Kit, damn it, let me down. *Now.*"

"Down now, Kit. Dammit!"

Lux snorted at his nephew's joyful mimicry. "Good man, Alexei. You tell that big, bad guardian who's boss."

"Don't encourage him." Zander closed his mouth with a snap, hand still curved around Kaine's shirt. "Thank you for bringing back my wayward family, Kit."

He turned his head, eyes narrowing on the guard in his grip. "It seems the person left in charge of protecting them was grabbing another sandwich from the larder instead of watching my son."

Kit inhaled slowly, setting Regina on her feet. "I apologize for that, sir."

He tried to hand the blond cherub in his arms to his mother, but Alexei grabbed onto Kit's slender braids and wouldn't let go. "Kaine will be reprimanded." The little imp patted his cheek soothingly, and Kit sent a bemused look toward the Mediator. "As soon as my hands are free."

"Kit! Dammit!"

Sylvain laughed delightedly, and Regina rolled her eyes, pulling the resisting bundle into her arms. "Sure, laugh now. It'll be my turn when you have *two* of these running around, starting little wind storms in the house, shape shifting when they don't want to take a bath."

Kit noticed Lux pale, looking to a nodding Zander for confirmation. "It gets worse. He is more like his mother than we thought he would be."

"He's a..." Zander nodded at the dumbfounded Lux. "But I thought only women could carry the Reader gene."

Nicolette, who'd been unusually silent for most of their journey, shrugged. "The Mother's Message was fulfilled. I do believe the old rulebook no longer applies. My appointment to the Trueblood council is proof of that."

Kit couldn't fault her logic. He had a feeling Liz knew exactly what she was doing by leaving the elegant courtesan in charge. The Madame held her passions in check so well, one would think her cold. But they would be wrong.

She was anything but, as they'd all just recently learned. Her cool hid her own thwarted passion for Arygon's late father, and the regret she felt at starting the long, drawn-out feud between the Devas and the

Dydarren Pack. It was a trait that would, no doubt, serve her well in the days to come.

The Clan Trust had never been a warm or welcoming crowd. And seeing an Unborn among their ranks would surely disturb some of the genetic puritans. Liz would have burned all her bridges before the end of the first meeting. She had no patience for the old ways. Nicolette, with her gentility and intelligence, not to mention the wholehearted endorsement of the Sariels, their Reader and the Were Alpha, would have them eating from the palm of her hand.

"You're right about that. Things have definitely changed for the better." Regina smiled over her son's curls, sending her husband that knowing glance Kit had seen her give so many times. That same look Lux and his two mates shared when they thought no one was looking. It was love.

How he envied them that.

The men released Kaine, who huffed and blustered, stepping toward the other side of the room, out of danger. "I knew they'd be fine. Even though Kit was with them."

Kit snarled, baring his fangs. "Be careful, Kaine, lest your words dig you a deeper pit." He stood taller, drawing the eye of everyone in the room. "Until I meet with the Old Ones, I still outrank you. Return home. Send Hibron in your stead."

Kaine choked on his sandwich at his brother's words. "*She* sent me here. She won't be happy with you for sending me back."

Kit knew he was speaking of their mother. "I'll deal with her soon enough. Go, Kaine. That's an order."

Jasyn growled low in his throat when Kaine seemed to hesitate. The large buffoon flinched and swooped to grab his sandwich before he left. "Fine. I didn't want to come here anyway. We shouldn't be bowing and scraping to anyone, not when we're—"

"There lies a dangerous road, brother. Don't go down it." Kit felt his head hit the arched ceiling, a small flurry of plaster falling around his shoulders. He'd begun to shift into his larger form, and he hadn't even been aware, too focused on his sibling. Kaine dangled in the air, clawing at Kit's large fist gripping his throat.

Damn his brother for making him lose his hard-won control. He unclenched his fingers, dropping the gasping dolt like a stone on the hard floor. "I won't tell you again, Kaine. Go home."

Kaine let out an angry roar, but he didn't challenge the command. He stood and turned to leave without a backward glance. Kit didn't move until his senses told him his brother was truly gone.

The silence was telling. Leave it to Kaine to single-handedly destroy the trust and respect he and the other guardians had built with the Sariels for thousands of years. How could his mother not see Kaine for what he was? Had she learned nothing?

He focused on calming down and returning to his normal size. Kit could only hope he hadn't frightened little Alexei. And that the Mediator would accept his apology.

"That was your *brother*? And I thought mine was a pain in the ass."

"Yours? What about mine?"

"I'd agree with you, but I don't want to be banished to the couch for the foreseeable future."

Kit swallowed his surprise, turning to watch Zander cross his arms at Lux and Jasyn's banter. "Smart move, my brother." He glanced over his shoulder at Kit. "They have a point though. No wonder you've never asked for any vacation time."

Kit shook his head, his gaze clashing with Max's, who seemed just as perplexed as he was at the vampire's reaction. This family continued to surprise him. No wonder Kit's sire had pledged his allegiance to them.

He felt a tug on his boots and looked to see Alexei beaming up at him with an expression of awed delight. "Again, Kit. Again!"

The lump in his throat had returned. He had to leave. The sooner the better.

Okay, so Ye Olde Haven Pub existed exactly where she'd thought it was going to be. And yes, it was the only one in the neighborhood that was closed until the sun went down. So what? That didn't mean it was owned and patronized by vampires. Vampires didn't exist.

Oh God, what if they were real?

Jesse clutched her small carryon and camera bag close, as if to shield her from that possibility. She breathed in and out slowly, regaining a measure of calm. She'd been in tight spots before. She'd been shot at by South American drug lords, threatened by embarrassed politicians. Once she had even been cornered by a seriously camera-shy alligator. Talk about fangs, that mouthful had given her nightmares for a month.

She could do this. She had to. Especially if her dreams the last few nights were anything to go by. He needed her. And time was growing short.

A small group, all dressed in black and giggling like teenagers, headed for the front entrance. Goth kids? In this sleepy town? Jesse smiled. That was more like it. Vampire wannabes, drinking goblets of red wine, pretending it was blood. Maybe that's what she'd been seeing. She held on to the relieving possibility and followed close behind them as they entered the pub. Haven.

"Wow."

"Told you this place was awesome. Wait until you get a load of the owner. He's delicious. Unfortunately he's married with a baby. But there's no shortage of hot, available men to donate to."

Jesse eavesdropped without apology, silently agreeing with the first girl's assessment. Wow, indeed. It was like they'd picked up a club in Soho and plopped it down in the middle of nowhere. The mixture of antique and modern, elegance and comfort made Jesse's trigger finger itchy. She wouldn't even need a flash. The lighting, the ambiance, was perfect. Even the char marks from the recent fire added to its charm.

Her Goth group headed onto the dance floor, drawing the gazes of the men and women lounging on leather couches against the wall.

Jesse stopped breathing as she studied them. They were flawless. All of them. Super models weren't this perfect until they'd been airbrushed. And their expressions as they watched the young group gyrating across the floor were easy to define. Hunger. Lust and hunger.

"Holy shit."

"Hello there. You're new aren't you? I think I would remember if I'd seen you before. You've got that sexy librarian look down to a T. I have a thing for librarians. Especially big, busty ones like you. You have magnificent breasts, darling. I would *never* have forgotten those."

Jesse pushed her glasses up the bridge of her nose, her expression indignant. She turned to give worst-pick-up-line-ever guy a piece of her mind, and nearly dropped her camera bag at the sight of him. Good Lord he was gorgeous. And he was the same height as she was. That didn't happen very often.

She didn't even like blonds, but this guy was hot as hell, and giving her a look that she was fairly certain could melt her panties right off her body.

"Um...thanks?" Thanks? Did she actually just use that breathy voice she despised in other women, thanking Mr. Sexpot for noticing her breasts?

His smile turned knowing. He leaned in, his mouth a breath away from her neck. "And a donation virgin as well? I would love to be the one to initiate you. This *is* your first time isn't it? Perhaps we should go someplace private. Donating can be a *very* pleasurable experience. Some women are a little shy about climaxing in front of strangers."

Donating? Climax? Alarm bells went off in her brain, jarring her out of the drooling daze she'd entered as soon as she saw him. "Actually..." She swallowed past the knot that suddenly developed in her throat. "Actually I think I'd rather pass...for now. But thank you for asking."

Mr. Sexpot looked disappointed, but he didn't press. "It's a shame. I bet you taste delicious. If you change your mind..." He moved off toward the dance floor in search of more willing company, and Jesse breathed a sigh of relief. There could be no doubt. That part of her vision was true as well. Vampires were real.

Well hell.

She walked over to the bar to order a drink. Hopefully they served vodka along with type AB positive. "Martini?" The pretty bartender nodded, pulling a glass from the rack without a word.

Jesse wasn't sure what to do. She had a feeling anyone snooping around beyond the main bar area, especially someone who was merely human, would be shown the door. Maybe that would be for the best. If she had a brain cell left in her head, she'd be running back to Heathrow as fast as her feet could take her.

She took a sip of her drink, spying over the rim of her glass a golden-eyed imp peeking around a door that only moments ago had looked like part of the wall. Pale ringlets swirled adorably around his head. His cheeks were rosy with laughter.

He must be the Mediator's child. She closed her eyes for a moment. It was disconcerting, the fact that she knew that. And what's more, the little scamp seemed to know her too. He was looking straight at her, hopping up and down as though he'd been waiting for her arrival.

Where were his parents? She looked around to see if anyone had noticed him and set down her drink. Jesse was fairly certain the Mediator and his wife would not like their little one seeing the make-out fest currently taking place on the dance floor.

She slid off her stool and walked over, bending down to his level. "I bet your mommy is looking for you. I'd say it's a little late for a baby like you to be up, but I think we both know that you're not the average toddler."

"Kit. Dammit."

Jesse felt her eyebrows climb to her hairline in shock. "What? Did you say Kit?" The little boy giggled and turned, running down the hallway to where she was sure was the owner's private domain. "Shit."

She looked over her shoulder. No one was paying any attention to her. Even the bartender had disappeared behind the bar. She peered into the darkness. "Shit." She slid through the narrow opening in the door, closing it behind her with a near silent click.

She couldn't see a thing. An eerie feeling replaced her concern and curiosity. But he'd said Kit's name. "Where'd you go? I don't have your super vision, buddy. I'm only human here."

"Which begs the question, what is a *human* doing chasing a helpless child into the darkness where she clearly doesn't belong?"

She could feel the heat of a large body beside her, the deep voice seeming to come from an impossible height. Was this the giant warrior of her dreams? "I-I saw him through th-the door and I—"

"You what? Saw an opportunity to take advantage? To steal something? Or perhaps your sexual proclivities weren't satisfied by the grown men outside?"

The disgust and judgment in his voice drove away her fear. "Listen up, you big bastard. I don't care *who* you are, you have no right to accuse me of something so perverted. I didn't think a baby should be wandering about in a bar, excuse me for living."

She put her hands on her hips, certain he could see her in the blackness. "And while we're on the subject, what were you doing sleeping on the job? Isn't it a Sariel guard's duty to keep the Mediator's family safe?"

The lights switched on, and Jesse covered her eyes, blinking as she tried to adjust to the bright light.

"Well, I like her. She has spunk. But don't blame him, my lovely. Alexei already has the skills of a first rate cat burglar. He's hard to keep track of."

Jesse looked up the stairs that had apparently been right beside her. It was them. All of them. In slow motion she tilted her head up to gaze at her accuser. “Oh. Hello, Max.”

Max took a surprised step back, and Jesse tried to hide her disappointment. “Lady, how do you know my name?”

She sighed. “It’s a long story.”

The man she recognized as Lux, who’d spoken for the group at the top of the stairs, smiled warmly in her direction. “That *is* good news. We love long stories. Max, bring the lady to our rooms. And for heaven’s sake quit looking so suspicious. Alexei is the one who let her in, and my nephew is nothing if not a great judge of character.”

Alexei clapped his hands in agreement, trying without success to wriggle out of the arms of his darkly exotic mother. She looked toward the tall blond male beside her and nodded. “Lux is right. Our son wanted her to follow him, but darned if I can get him to tell me why.”

They turned toward Jesse with open curiosity, and she allowed Max to direct her up the stairs.

This was surreal. The logical part of her brain was busy making lists of reasons why this couldn’t be real. Perhaps she’d fallen asleep on the plane, and this was yet another dream.

With every moment that passed, however, it became more and more apparent that her dreams hadn’t been dreams at all. Not in the normal sense of the word. She knew these people. She'd watched their courtships, seen them face dangers that could hardly be believed. She'd seen it all through his eyes. Now here they all were. Everyone but him. Where *was* he?

She followed them into what seemed to be one large loft apartment. The building looked smaller on the outside. "You've made some changes since the fire." The blurted words stopped everyone in their tracks.

Even the easygoing Lux seemed thrown. "Do we *know* you?"

"No. But she knows us. Don't you, *Jesse*?" The small, impossibly beautiful woman handed her child to her husband and walked closer.

Jesse noticed the black bindu marking the middle of her forehead, the silver streak in her ebony hair and smiled in bemusement. "Yes, Reggie the Reader. Apparently I do."

The men moved closer, alert to any danger she may represent to their family, and Jesse held up her hands defensively. "I thought you were a dream. A long, scary, detailed dream. But you're real. You're all real. My God, I need another drink."

Someone led her to a chair, and she heard the tinkling of ice before a drink was shoved into her hand. The little towheaded child waddled up and placed his cheek on her thigh, smiling at her. "Kit. Dammit."

Jesse chuckled morosely, patting his head as she sipped her drink. "That's right, buddy. Kit. Damn it."

"Kit? What about Kit...Jesse, is it?" Jesse nodded at Lux, whose voice had gentled as if he were calming a skittish colt.

"Yes. He's the reason I'm here. The reason I knew Haven existed. Why I know more about your lives than my own brother's."

"*Lies.* Kit would never tell *any* human, no matter how attractive, about the Sariels. He would die before he broke his vows." Max stood tall, trying to intimidate her, but Jesse just raised one brow.

"Max, cousin of Kit. You don't talk much but you're incredibly loyal, and your father is in charge of training warriors for the Sariel guard." She turned to the others. "Lux Sariel, youngest son of the Sariel family and a healer. You were a wild man until one of your lovers was killed by that psycho Grey Wolf, and then you met and mated Sylvain and that one's brother." Jesse waved toward Jasyn.

She smiled fondly at Sylvain's belly. "You have the ability to control nature, and you're pregnant with twins. They should be due any day now I'd imagine. And finally," Jesse shared a twinkling gaze with the little boy beside her. "Alexei. Firstborn son of a powerful telepath and the Mediator of the old stuffy vampire clans. He just might be the cutest little guy on the planet." She looked around. "The woman from the Deva clan must be out for the evening. Am I right?"

The men were looking at her as though she'd just sprouted horns and a tail. Sylvain and Regina, on the other hand, came closer, fascinated. "Kit didn't tell you this." Regina's tone was certain.

"Not exactly. I told you, I thought I dreamt it. My personal obsession with urban fantasy erotica, or those movies with vampires and werewolves fighting each other in skintight leather."

Sylvain and Regina nodded, crinkling their noses to show how they felt about the movies in question. Jesse snorted. "Exactly. I came to prove that none of this, none of you, existed. Because if you didn't exist, *he* wouldn't exist, and this terrible feeling I have could be chalked up to my overactive imagination."

But they did. And he did. And that could only mean... "Where's Kit?"

"You know every other damn thing, why don't you know that too?" Max ran a hand through his long dark hair. He looked familiar to her, and too much like Kit for her peace of mind. He also looked upset.

"He left already didn't he? I have to find him." She stood quickly, feeling a wave of dizziness crash over her. "I'm sorry. I must have jet lag or something. I feel strange."

Max turned her toward him, gripping her arms while studying her dilating pupils. "No, my lady. I'm afraid it's not jet lag. I drugged you."

He ignored the loud protests around him, as well as Alexei's tears, and leaned closer. "If you know me as you say you do, you know I only do what I must. We have to find out how much the Sariels have been compromised."

Jesse sensed the darkness creeping in, and her words were slurred. “Coulda just asked me. Need to find Kit. Need to...to...need to lie down.”

He shook her. “Why? Why is it so important to find him?”

Lux pulled her away from the adamant guard, lifting her in his arms to carry her to the bed. “What the hell is this, Max? No one gave you authorization to harm her.”

“You shouldn’t carry me. I’m too heavy.”

Lux made a soothing noise, shaking his head. “You *are* a tall one, but trust me, you feel like a feather in my arms. I’m sorry about this, love.”

Jesse patted Lux with a limp hand. “S’okay. It’s the training. They train a lot. Lux, I don’t know why, but Kit’s in here.” She pointed to her temple as he set her down. “In here and he needs me.”

She started to panic with the growing blackness. “Please listen to me. I don’t...want him to die...alone.”

Chapter Three

She found him sitting amidst the ruins of an old castle. "The Sariels are all at Haven. And they're worried about you. What are you doing here?"

Kit's lack of surprise in seeing her told her this must be another dream. He shrugged. "Believe it or not, I was just thinking about you. And how upset I was that we didn't finish what we started the other night."

He stood up. "They shouldn't worry. I can take care of myself. I was just saying goodbye to all my old haunts before I started for home."

"Oh. This is where Grey Wolf—"

"I don't want to dredge up bad memories. Not with you." He strode toward her, lifting her up onto a fallen column and, bending down until his lips stopped just short of hers. "You're the Mother's gift to me. My very own angel. With you, the only thing I want is this."

Jesse wanted desperately to talk to him, to tell him that his cousin had drugged her, that if he would stop daydreaming and come to the pub, he could see her in the flesh. But as usual, the moment he kissed her, she couldn't think of anything else.

She loved these, the dreams where it was just the two of them. When he touched her like this. Too often she would find herself viewing the dreamscape from behind his eyes, in his thoughts, experiencing everything he was. But this, this was what she lived for.

“Ah, angel, why do you always do this? Pretend that you are mousy and plain? I like you better in your nightshirt. And out of it.” Kit slid her hair out of its haphazard bun, releasing it to fall around her shoulders and down her back. “You shouldn’t hide this kind of beauty. It’s like wildfire in my hands.”

“I *am* mousy and plain. You only like my hair because it’s like hers.” Damn her mouth. She didn’t want to destroy this moment. She wanted his hands in her hair, on her skin. But she couldn’t help thinking about the woman he’d been with for nearly a year.

“You already know that’s not true.” He dipped his head to catch her gaze. “Elizabeth’s hair is *similar* to yours. But nothing can compare with this. This is perfection.”

She knew. Even during those terrible glimpses of them together, she knew his relationship with the founder of the Deva Clan had never been serious. For either of them. And she knew he couldn’t help thinking of her when he had been with Liz. Wrong as it was, the knowledge had given her comfort. But she needed more.

“Prove it.” Jesse reached up onto her tiptoes and wrapped her arms around his neck to pull him down for another kiss. She opened her mouth, her tongue sliding across his lips.

His low moan vibrated against her chest, hardening her nipples and sending delicious shivers along her spine. "Getting pretty sassy for such a little thing, aren't you, angel. You want proof? I think it's time I showed you once and for all." Kit cupped her ass with his large hands and nudged the ridge of his erection between her legs.

"Oh God, that sounds good. But..." She was overwhelmed with the sheer size of him. Ever since she'd been old enough to understand her attraction, she'd wanted him. He was the only man who'd ever made her feel feminine. Small. Being a sturdy six feet tall since she'd turned fifteen, that was saying something.

He read her silence. "Oh we'll fit quite nicely, *sarasvatti.* Trust me. This is my fantasy after all. And even though it has to end, I find I want to experience everything. To revel in you as long as I can. Say yes, angel. Tell me again what you want me to do. How you want me to fuck you."

Lord, she loved it when he called her that. "Yes."

The cool air hit her skin, and she smiled. "That old Trueblood trick?"

He chuckled at her comment, lowering a now naked Jesse to the grass and kneeling above her. "Who do you think taught it to them, love?" Kit's smile showed a glint of fang, and she trembled. It struck her again that he was real. This impossible myth of a man was real.

"Kit, I need to tell you something."

He spread her legs, placing them over his bare thighs, and shook his head slowly. "Talking later. Tasting now." His hair fell like a curtain around her, blocking out the night sky until all she could see were those eyes. Exotic, dark and decidedly not human.

Kit nibbled gently on her upper lip, smiling when she gasped at the sensation of his cock sliding against her wet sex. He battled lightly with her tongue, and she groaned in denial when he abandoned her mouth to lap at her chin, her shoulder, her neck.

"Goddess, I love the feel of your breasts in my hands. Your body is soft and lush, angel. Would that you were real. I could spend a lifetime feasting, and it would never be enough."

He didn't wait for her response, taking a nipple between his teeth and tugging hard. Jesse arched her back with a cry, loving the sharp sting, greedy for more. Kit's laugh was dark and low as he lifted his head. "Ah, yes. I know you. Know my angel likes a little pain with her pleasure. I remember how surprised you were the first time I made you come."

Jesse closed her eyes to his knowing gaze. She remembered too. "You spanked me."

He rewarded her words with a devilish lick along the underside of her breast. "You were driving me crazy. All grown up and determined to tease me into insanity. I didn't want to hurt you—"

"You didn't," she assured him, recalling how she'd loved it, how she had begged for more and arched up as much as she could with her jeans around her knees. How hard she'd come when his palm came down between her legs.

Kit seemed to be remembering it too. His hand left her breast and he shifted, lifting his body away from hers. The first smack against her pussy nearly lifted her off the ground in reaction. "Shit."

"Bad girl." Kit tsked, cupping his hand against her sex, slipping his thick middle finger deep inside. "And wet already. For *me*. Only for me. Say it."

She bit her lip, her entire being focused on his finger thrusting inside her. His other hand came down with a loud slap against her clit and she screamed, a heartbeat away from climax. He pulled both hands away and she opened her eyes in disbelief.

Kit made a show of licking his finger, long lashes lowering over those fathomless eyes. "Say it."

Jesse's thoughts raced. Say what? She'd forgotten what they were talking about, but she'd say anything to have him touch her again. "Only you, Kit. I only want you."

One more spank against her pussy lips and she was coming, crying out his name. He growled his approval. Lifting her hips off the ground and her legs over his shoulders, he opened her to his avid gaze. "That's right, my angel. Come for me. Let me taste it. Feed me."

He lapped at her thighs, following the damp trail of her arousal to the lips of her sex. His thorough tongue traced her pussy lips, a continuous purr of pleasure rumbling from his chest as he drank her in.

His lips closed over her clit, sucking hard while his two fingers pressed inside her tight sheath. Jesse felt tears gather at the corners of her eyes as another, smaller quake followed the first. And she hadn't even gotten to touch him yet. "Kit, please."

He lifted his head, full lips damp with her juices, and she had to kiss him. To taste herself on his tongue. He must have read the need in her gaze, because he leaned over her body, pressing her knees back toward her shoulders while he ate at her mouth.

She was out of control, unable to get close enough. "Kit. Oh God, Kit. I want…I want…"

"I know what you want, *sarasvatti*. It's all I've been able to think about for years. Being inside you. Finally where I belong."

"Oh my."

Disorientation blurred her vision as Kit leapt up to a standing position, holding Jesse's naked body protectively against his chest. "What in the name of—Priestess Magriel?"

Jesse tilted her head at an impossible angle, until she was looking at the upside-down image of two women hiding behind a nearby tree. One of them looked incredibly familiar. And she was blushing. "Reggie?"

She sat bolt upright with a gasp. She was in a large, decadent bed. Still fully clothed, but sporting one hell of a headache. Regina and an older, tattooed woman she knew instantly was the Healer Glynn Magriel were sitting on either side of her, both holding their own heads as though feeling her pain. It came back to her with a jolt. "You *drugged* me."

Regina reached out to take her hand. "No, Jesse. We had no idea Max was going to do that. He said he was just following protocol. Apparently a human knowing as much as you seemed to, and claiming a Sariel guard was the source of your information, is a serious accusation."

Jesse rubbed her temples. Inwardly cringing as she recalled the last few moments she'd shared with Kit. She caught Regina's blushing gaze and knew. "You were watching us. Both of you."

Glynn Magriel nodded serenely, though Jesse could see a definite twinkle in her eyes. "Of course we were. It was the only way we could find out how you knew so much. As well as allowing us to tell our guard here that Kit is not a traitor to his people, and his family line will not be branded for eternity with dishonor and everlasting damnation."

The last was said with just enough sarcasm to make Max shuffle uncomfortably from his post at the foot of the bed. Jesse marveled. Hard as it was to believe, they were still here. Still real. And she had walked, voluntarily, into the lair of beings usually relegated to nightmares and scary movies. Although, for bloodsucking fiends, they looked quite domesticated.

Lux was holding a tired Sylvain on his lap, her head resting sweetly in the crook of his neck. Jasyn and Zander Sariel were talking in hushed voices over a table laden with food. And the tall, elegant Deva, Nicolette, was cuddled with little Alexei beside the fire. From the expressive movement of her hands and his rapt expression, she decided the Unborn was weaving a fairly interesting yarn.

"Did you find what you were looking for?" Jesse threw her legs over the bed, looking for her bags. She needed to find her way out of here.

"If my *grathita*'s state of arousal is anything to go by, they found more than they were looking for." Zander pulled his wife off the bed and into his arms. "Well, my *priya*? Should I be jealous?"

Jesse noticed for the first time that Regina was flushed with more than just embarrassment. She was aroused, and giving her husband a look so intimate that no one in the room could fail to feel its heat. Oh for heaven's sake. Her dreams were Reader porn.

The priestess chuckled as though she'd read her thoughts, pulling Jesse's gaze away from the passionate couple. "We really didn't mean to pry into your private time, dear. But the dream was so vivid we could do little more than walk inside it and observe. That is one powerful ability you have."

Jesse found her glasses on the side table and slipped them on, a nervous sound escaping her throat. "I think it's safe to say I'm the one person in this room with no special powers of any kind. I'm just an ordinary human, remember?"

"Hardly ordinary, dear. And I rarely say things I don't mean. It's powerful, all right. I'm just not entirely sure *why* you have it."

Jesse looked back at Regina, who nodded against her husband's chest. "Neither Glynn nor I sensed any Reader abilities in you, but the link was definitely initiated on your end."

Max looked relieved. "So Kit...?"

"He believes I'm a figment of his imagination." Jesse felt her shoulders slump. After seeing Max's reaction, she'd begun to wonder if maybe that wasn't a good thing. She knew Kit better than most. That was the problem. He wouldn't appreciate the fact that someone had been mucking around his head without his knowledge. There was a sudden sick feeling in her heart. He would hate her.

"One of you should probably put me in that thrall thingy. Convince me the pub doesn't exist, that I discovered everything was a dream, and then I can go home and find a nice boring accountant to date." Jesse slid her camera bag over her shoulder and held her overnight bag against her churning stomach.

"What about Kit, my lady? You were fairly adamant that he was in danger. That you had to get to him. Has that changed?"

No, it hadn't. With every second that passed, she needed to be with him more. Whatever he was about to face, she couldn't shake the feeling that he needed her.

But what could she possibly do to help him? She shook her head at Lux. "He has all of you, whether he knows it or not. He doesn't need some strange human following him around. Besides, from all I've seen, your goddess will protect him."

"No." Max lifted his chin, not looking anyone in the eye when they turned toward him, startled. "The Mother will not help him this time. She cannot. It is the law."

"I am close to losing my patience with you, Max. First, you drug a guest in my home without my permission, now you speak in riddles and blaspheme in the presence of my child. Explain yourself."

Max came to attention, bowing respectfully to Zander, his eyes distraught. "Please do not ask that of me, Mediator. I must show allegiance to my people, even before my vow to your family." He glanced at Jesse. "I meant no blasphemy. The Great Mother herself knows the law. She was there when it was written."

"Is anybody else dying of curiosity? Sylvain, if Max won't tell us what he's talking about, what did you and Lux see in your dreamwalk?" Jasyn stood beside his brother's mates, both of them gazing intently at the Sariel guard.

Sylvain cupped her engorged belly protectively. "The Mother was distraught. We could sense it. All we saw were disjointed images. A desert, ancient ruins, a great mountain. Kit was in every one of them, and in each one, he was suffering. We woke feeling he would never return."

Lux pulled Sylvain close, both obviously disturbed by the memory.

Max had gone pale, his body trembling with suppressed knowledge. Jesse had had enough. “You’re his cousin. I know how you feel about him, how much you’ve been through. Surely whatever mission he’s being sent on, *you* can join him, keep him safe.”

He shook his head. “The Old Ones would never choose me to be his witness. I am highest in rank, after him. I’m needed here. But, they will choose someone to go with him. He’ll not be alone.”

“I hate this.” Regina pulled out of her husband’s embrace, pacing the room in a sensual feline way that Jesse could only envy. “All this secrecy, these protocols...I know you can’t tell us where Kit is going, but is there *nothing* we can do?”

“He can take Jesse to his people’s settlement and inform the Old Ones of her security breach, as verified by the Priestess Magriel.” Glynn stood, her long, silver hair falling over her shoulders, blue spiral tattoos glowing in the soft light.

Jesse didn’t like where this was going. “I’m sure they would love to see me. I bet I would even get to be the guest of honor at dinner. Nestled between the new potatoes and suckling pig.”

The Sariel guard jerked as though physically struck by Jesse’s words. He gave a tense nod to Glynn. “Bringing her in front of my people is what my training would demand.”

Max folded his arms, the barest hint of a smirk crossing his stony features. "The human *did* say she wanted to find Kit. There is no doubt he will be there by sunrise. But I'm afraid I could not vouch for her safety. I am not sure how the Old Ones will react."

The room turned to chaos.

Regina and Lux whirled on Glynn Magriel, disbelief in their voices as they argued against simply handing her over. They were fighting like dogs over a bone.

Jesse did *not* want to be the bone in this scenario. She was about to bolt for the door while everyone was distracted, when a calm Jasyn silenced the cacophony. "I'll go with them. I'm no guard, but at least she would have a fighting chance."

Glynn Magriel appeared at Jesse's shoulder, grabbing her hand. "We have no more time to lose. The guard Kit requested arrived this evening. Max, you will go with Jasyn and Jesse and deliver your charges." She looked over the concerned faces without softening her tone.

"We must trust in the Mother. Jesse was sent with a power that we've yet to encounter. She came determined to find Kit. Just because we do not know this road, doesn't mean we avoid the journey."

Jesse felt a wave of warmth and comfort coming from the priestess. She was right. Jesse had come because Kit needed her. Whether he knew it or not. And damn it, after all this, he'd better be the same man he was in her dreams. If not, well, there were plenty other sexy, giant immortals in the world. Yeah. Sure there were.

"You blinked." Kit held out his hand to the man lying on the ground. It was taken grudgingly, the arrogant student embarrassed in front of his friends by the far superior Sariel guard.

"You, all of you, lack focus." Kit set down his staff, pacing slowly in front of the line of warriors. "Shadow stalking, for all its advantages, makes you physically weaker. More importantly, when you are called on to protect and defend, you will not be able to retain that gift from the Mother. You have to be seen to effectively battle the enemy. And you have to be good to win."

He stopped in front of a warrior that had shifted to his larger size, towering above the others. Kit was unfazed. "Neither is your sheer size enough. You must know how to fight with every weapon in your arsenal. Your sword, your staff, your size. Above all these, your wits will be your greatest ally."

Kit started moving once more, enumerating the potential threats on his fingers. "Vampires can thrall you. They can transform into anything from a small bird to a slippery snake. Weres are stronger than you imagine, craftier and savage in their shifted form. Without training, our kind are clumsy, distracted. That is a weakness you cannot afford as a Sariel guard."

Before he could continue, he was interrupted. "My brother fills your head with the same nonsense your Master Trainer spouts. Our natural speed, size and ability to walk unseen through the world makes us superior to any creature walking the Earth. *Any* creature. Even the much praised members of the Sariel Clan. True weakness is lining up to run decade-long drills instead of enjoying your powers. A fact the Trueblood's pet Kitty doesn't understand."

The students shuffled uncomfortably, some smirking, a few rolling their eyes. Kit smiled. He'd known it was only a matter of time before Kaine felt safe enough to confront him. He lifted his staff and tossed it at his brother's feet. "Kaine. I accept your challenge. And to make it a fair fight..." He unhooked his sword belt and opened his palms, showing he had no weapons.

The men gathered around them froze at the action. There was no greater insult to a warrior than to imply he had no chance of winning without unfair advantage. Kaine, however, only smiled, reaching for the bullwhip looped at his hip, the only weapon he'd ever shown proficiency with. He cracked it loudly across the space dividing them. Showing off, more a circus performer than a warrior. He was a fool.

They circled each other warily, two male animals squaring off. Kaine's lips curled back, revealing yellow teeth as his fangs, both upper and lower, extended. "I've waited centuries to watch you bleed. But don't worry. I won't kill you. She says you need to stay alive. For now."

"A mother's love. It warms the heart. And it's good to see her baby boy still willing to do anything Mommy says."

"Bastard." Kaine lashed out with the whip, his intent clear, but he missed Kit by a mile.

"Pay attention, men. Anger is the enemy of skill. If my brother actually had any to begin with, his emotions would have overridden his training."

Kaine's face grew dark with humiliation as the others laughed. Kit smirked, but he remained alert. His brother's anger was bubbling to the surface, showing in the stretching of his features, the enlarging of bones and the sound of his clothes tearing as he slowly shifted into a larger form.

He was just as clumsy at shifting as he was with everything else. A Were had the instinctive ability to transform into their beast, though most didn't start until a few years after their birth. Truebloods and Unborns had the ability to transform into an animal befitting their spirit. To them it came as easy as breathing, once they learned how.

His people had always had the ability, but as with everything, without the proper discipline to control the process, it became more of a hindrance than an advantage. Kit spun low to the ground, using his lower center of gravity to sweep Kaine's thickening legs out from under him. He fell with a booming thud, splintering an adolescent pine beneath him as he dropped.

"And that's why size is no guarantee you've won the battle."

Kaine lumbered to his feet, his size now doubling Kit's. "I'll grind you into the dirt and—"

"What? Use my bones to bake your bread? Don't be a human's cliché, Kaine. Enough talk, you've interrupted the real warriors from their training long enough."

As he moved, he knew that the students would see what he'd seen Max's father do a thousand times. A blur of speed and power that surpassed the oldest Trueblood, the largest of his kind. But it wasn't that he was moving faster. It was only time, slowing down.

The Master had seen it in him all those years ago, the ability so few of them possessed. Shadow stalking was a gift from the Mother goddess to all of his people, their salvation. But a precious few could look beyond the shadow space, could balance along the thin thread of time and bend it to their will. Not forever, just enough to be invaluable in battle.

Kit looked around to see the world had taken on a grayish tint. Grainy, like an old roll of film. All the men around him were staring at the point where he'd started, their jaws frozen mid-drop.

He tilted his head toward Kaine and sighed. There was a time, thousands of years ago when they first arrived on this cold, wet island, that he'd loved his brother. He coddled him as his mother did, took him under his wing, despite their father's impatience with his youngest son's proclivities.

Ultimately, it was Kaine's jealousy, carefully cultivated and grown by their mother that had shattered any trace of a brotherly bond between them. Kit saw the gleam of pure hatred in Kaine's eyes, and he knew that

Kaine would kill him if he could. And he would eat hardy and sleep soundly with no regrets. His mother had created a monster. Father had been right all along.

Kit shook away the sadness, concentrating on maintaining his focus. He pulled the whip out of his brother's hands, his own moving swiftly as he did what he had to do to bring this scuffle to an end.

He blinked, and the world filled with color once more. Kaine wobbled dangerously, before falling once again, this time directly into the scattering crowd. When the others realized why he had fallen, the crowd began to roar with laughter. Kaine snarled at them, legs wriggling in the dirt as he struggled to release himself. Kit knew his brother would have to return to his average size if he wanted to regain circulation from where the whip had been knotted around his ankles.

"You shamed him. He won't be able to let this go."

Kit nodded, turning to face his trainer and mentor, Master Elam, Max's father. "You're right, Master. But between this moment and tomorrow's audience, there is not much he can do. And why would he want to when he'll enjoy what's coming much more than any petty vengeance he could devise?"

Elam swore, his anger and frustration readily apparent. "It hasn't happened yet. Come with me, I've convinced one of the Old Ones to talk to us in private, and I doubt you'll get any more training in today."

Kit glanced over his shoulder. He had a point. His students had disbanded, some of them attempting to calm the raging Kaine, but most crowing over Kit's amazing feat. Nothing else would be learned today.

They began walking down the path that would lead them into the settlement. Kit was about to ask him who they were going to meet, when a strange sensation washed over his body. Kit stepped in front of Elam when the bushes off to the right of them rustled.

He inhaled deeply, and several scents surrounded him. Two of them were familiar but unexpected. The third? The third was too unacceptable to be believed. "Max, Jasyn, who have you brought with you? And why didn't you take the main path?"

But it wasn't Max or the Were Beta who emerged from the brush.

It was her.

She looked frightened and tired, and more beautiful than anything he'd seen in his life. But why were her wrists tied in front of her like a prisoner? "*Sarasvatti*?"

"Kit." Her smile was tremulous, hopeful. He understood the feeling well. She was real? His angel was real? And she was here, a human, in his people's secured settlement.

"I hate to disturb this happy reunion, but Max seems to believe that Jesse should be hidden as quickly as possible until your elders can be told about her. After seeing the tail end of that sibling smack down, I would tend to agree."

Jasyn appeared behind her, his arm wrapping around her shoulders in a supportive squeeze. Kit narrowed his eyes dangerously. Max stepped in front of both of them, blocking his view. "Father. Kit."

"Have you gone mad, boy? The Beta can be explained, perhaps even forgiven through his connection to the Sariels, but a human? Humans are not welcome here. We cannot protect her from the warriors. We certainly cannot allow her to leave with the knowledge of our location. What were you thinking, Maximus?" Elam's words were hushed and utterly confused.

Max's expression as he looked at Kit spoke volumes. Disappointment. Shame. And regret. "She knows about us, Father. She knows about the Sariels. The Weres. Everything. She's here to be brought before the Old Ones that they may decide her fate."

"How?"

Kit flinched as Max uttered the truth that moments earlier had hit him like an avalanche. "Kit has been compromised."

Chapter Four

"Filthy, rotten, son of a bitch *bastard.*"

"Wow. And you were so quiet on the way here."

Jesse turned to find Jasyn leaning against the open doorway of the cave-*cum*-prison cell Max had stuck her in. The candles lit on copper fixtures in the rough hewn walls were the only light in the dank cave, but she could see enough to know that no one had been here in a very long time. Long enough for whatever was rustling in the corner to move in. She shuddered, pulling the fur blanket they'd thrown in tightly around herself.

"Swearing keeps me from freezing to death. Thanks for the help, Dydarren. I thought you came to protect me, not stand by and watch as I'm tossed into a pit to rot by a grumpy warrior with a Dudley Do-Right complex."

Jasyn sighed. "Jesse, please. Max had no other choice. I believe him when he says this is the safest place you can be. Even with how careful we were, they still sensed your presence. Elam, Kit and Max are all outside in order to ensure your protection."

He lowered his voice. "Honestly, I had no idea this place was even here. That there were more than a handful of Sariel guards in existence. There were stories, most of them too farfetched for anyone to believe. All we were ever told about Kit's people was that they were different. Powerful, old and utterly loyal to the Mediator's family. A blood oath, Lux said. But I don't think anyone, even the Sariels, have stepped foot in this fortress of a settlement before. Did you see it when we came in? It's incredible."

It was. A valley hidden by endless fog. A giant city built into a Scottish mountainside. Ironically, she'd taken photos of this range for a travel magazine years ago. The Black Cuillin range on the Isle of Skye. Jesse had fallen in love with the rough, breathtaking landscape. She'd wanted to come back ever since. Only not as a prisoner.

How had they stayed hidden for so long? The British Isles were small and crowded, the mountain ranges anthills in comparison to most. Yet they not only lived here, they'd hewn a masterpiece of craftsmanship out of the rock. Columns of rock, smoothed and polished. Villas floating against the mountain's face, connected by a series of giant, spiral steps. It was magnificent. Enchanted.

This was Kit's home. She'd never seen it before, not in any of her visions of him. But it was easy to imagine him here, among all this majesty in the mist. It hit her again, like a sucker punch to the gut. He was actually here. A few feet away.

Ignoring her.

"He didn't even talk to me, Jasyn. I know he recognized me. But after that first..." She turned her back, unwilling to show how deeply Kit's silence had hurt her.

Jasyn's hands cupped her shoulders through the blanket, pulling her into a friendly embrace. "I wish I could help you, but I'm not the one to turn to for advice about romance."

Jesse sniffled. "I know you believe that. And even I have to admit, when it comes to Hannah, you have issues. It wasn't her fault you know. She didn't asked to be turned, and you weren't around to save her. Would you really rather she'd have died that night?"

He froze, his fingers tightening over her shoulders until she squeaked in pain. He pulled back to look into her eyes. "I'm sorry. I forgot how much you know. But there is more to it than you could understand. Too much water under the bridge."

"You love each other. Nothing's changed that." She didn't understand these people. They were given amazing abilities, unimaginably long lives, and they wasted it with miscommunications and petty jealousies. They saw forever, but were blind to what was right in front of them. She sighed. In that way she guessed they weren't so different from humans after all.

"Beta Dydarren, you should go."

Jesse jumped away from the kind Were to face the new arrival. Kit. He didn't take his dark eyes from Jasyn, his expression hard and unyielding. More frightening than she remembered.

Jasyn didn't move. "I took an oath to keep her safe. Max vowed to protect her until she met with the Old Ones. *You* made no such promise. Why would I leave her alone with you?"

Kit took a step forward. "You know me. I would never hurt an innocent. If you need an oath consider it given and go, or I will make another promise. That my fondness for you will not save you if you don't take your hands off of her and join Max and his father outside."

"Oh brother." Jesse stepped between the two men, turning to Jasyn. "Go, please. Just...not too far."

Jasyn winked at her, giving Kit a wide berth as he disappeared around the corner. She tilted her head, studying him as he stared at a point over her shoulder. She wasn't going to beg. If he didn't want to talk to her, didn't have anything to say to her after all these years, all they'd shared then—

"Jesse." God, his voice was sexy. "You never told me your name was Jesse."

"You never asked."

Kit nodded, his expression impossible to read. He bent, setting a large leather satchel on the floor and untying the closure. "Elam's wife brought you something to eat. Max said he pushed you hard to get here."

Her stomach growled at the mention of food. Some restaurant crackers and a candy bar she kept in her camera bag for emergencies was all she'd eaten in the day it had taken to get here. Jasyn had mentioned they would have arrived faster, but they weren't used to traveling with humans. "That was kind of her. I guess even hardened criminals get a last meal."

The cloth-wrapped plates clattered to the floor. Kit didn't look up. "Did Max hurt you before you arrived?"

Jesse reached for one of the hot buttered rolls he was revealing, her stomach overruling her nerves. "You mean other than thinking I was trying to snatch Alexei for some nefarious purpose, drugging me and then bringing me to this farce of a trial where God knows what will happen instead of letting me go home?"

Kit's fingers wrapped around her forearm, their heat scalding as he turned her arm over to inspect her wrist. It was still a little red, but she knew that he'd been expecting far worse. She knelt beside him. "He didn't tie me until we entered the settlement. It was just protocol. Not cruelty."

The dreams had been so real. The desire she'd felt in them unbelievable in its intensity. But none of that compared with this simple touch. His fingers, rough from a life of war and labor, traced her palm, the hint of veins along her wrist. She inhaled, leaning to drink him in with all her senses. Just for a moment to revel in his existence, then she'd find her anger again.

He pulled back, moving to sit on the floor against the far wall. "Eat." And wham, the anger returned. Jesse rolled her eyes, plopping on the dirty ground and sitting Indian style before grabbing her plate. The woman had made enough to feed an army. Or one seven-foot Neanderthal.

Thankfully it wasn't anything unusual. The plate held a leg of lamb, and some carrots and potatoes along with the rolls. She'd pictured haggis with a side of screaming village peasant. Jesses chuckled to herself and slipped a tender piece of lamb between her lips.

"You aren't a Reader, Priestess Magriel would have sensed it."

Jesse nodded while she chewed, swallowing before she answered. "That's right. I'm just your garden variety human, apart from..." She gestured toward him with a chunk of roll, blushing before shoving it in her mouth.

She nervously licked the butter off her lips, reaching for the container of water she'd seen sticking out of the satchel. She blushed when she noticed Kit's gaze fixed, unblinking, on her lips as she ate.

Her body warmed under his gaze. Suddenly the blanket was too hot, too confining. She shrugged it off until it fell around her waist, and then took another large gulp of water. The low moan she heard had her spilling some of the water down her chin and onto her shirt. Great. Very graceful.

She heard it again. It sounded pained. And then she was being grabbed, as though she weighed nothing, and pressed against the smooth rock wall. Kit's chest rose and fell swiftly against hers, his expression haunted as he pressed against her.

Her feet were dangling in the air, arms trapped at her sides where he held her. She felt off balance, out of control. Instinctively she wrapped her legs around his waist.

"Fuck, angel, I... Great Mother you feel..." Kit dropped his forehead to the wall beside her. His hips ground against her, his erection hard and hot between her thighs. Was this really happening? She would shatter if she woke up alone in her bedroom. Again.

"Is this another dream?"

Kit let go of her arms and cupped her ass in his hands, pumping his cock against her. She groaned aloud, frantic to feel more, to feel him inside of her. "I don't think so. If this was a dream I could hold back. Or wake up before I went too far."

He slid a hand between them and unzipped her jeans, popping the top button so it skidded across the floor. His fingers sifted through the curls protecting her sex and tugged, making her gasp and arch into his hand. "I'd make you come with my mouth and hands until you were boneless in my arms. But I'd never take you. If this were a dream, the dream I've been having for so many years, I wouldn't get to feel *this*—" he slid two fingers inside her soaking pussy and growled, "—squeezing around my cock like a fist as I come."

Jesse nearly cried out when their clothes disappeared, and she felt him naked against her. He silenced her with his lips, pulling back far enough to whisper. "Shh, *sarasvatti*. This isn't a dream. And three warriors who are definitely *not* human are right outside. Their senses, like mine, are more heightened than you would imagine. They can pretend they don't smell the scent of your desire, growing stronger, richer, with every passing moment. But they won't be able to ignore your screams."

"Oh God." Instead of frightening her, the knowledge increased her arousal. And he knew. His nostrils flared as he breathed her scent in, lips lifting in a silent snarl that revealed his extending fangs.

"No point in praying, angel. I've tried. Taking you goes against every code of my kind. And I believe in that code. So strongly that I denied myself, even when I thought you weren't real. But I can't bring myself to care anymore. Not now. Not when you're here in front of me. All I can think of is fucking you." Kit lifted her with his palms, spreading her ass cheeks and angling her hips until she could feel the wide head of his cock align with her sex.

No alarm rang. Her sister-in-law wasn't on the phone. There was nothing to stop him as he pressed slowly inside. He was so thick, so big she wasn't sure she could take him. Her head burrowed into the crook of his neck, mouth opening over his shoulder to conceal her moans. Her muscles clung tightly to his shaft, making him fight for every inch.

"Jesse, baby, look at me, please." She lifted her head, her body trembling uncontrollably against his. He wasn't faring much better. "I can't wait any longer, angel, but I don't want to hurt you. It doesn't matter how many human men you've been with, my people are—"

"I haven't." His long lashes fell as his eyes closed, making it easier for her to continue. "I haven't been with anyone else. Human or other." She wiggled against him experimentally, her body struggling to accommodate his girth. His fingers tightened on her ass, stopping her movement.

"Why?"

She kissed his chin, loving the strong touch. "No ordinary man could compare with my dreams."

He jerked, shuddering against her. "*Sarasvatti. My* angel. Only mine." He took a deep breath. "I'm going to bite you, Jesse. Not like a Trueblood or a Were bite, I can't make you what I am. But I can help your body relax, help you take all of me."

Jesse lifted her head, eyes wide behind her glasses, and Kit smiled darkly. "Don't worry, my kinky little goddess. You'll still feel the sting. Still feel the stretch. But you'll feel pleasure as well. More pleasure than you've ever imagined."

She was breathless. "I've imagined a lot."

He chuckled, reading the answer in her eyes. He kissed her softly, nibbling at her lips lightly, teasingly. His tongue lowered, lingering on her collarbone, tracing the smattering of freckles along her chest. "These breasts, angel. I thought my mind had fashioned them just for me—lush and heavy cream, topped with dark raspberry nipples begging for my touch. They are the perfect confection for a ravenous man."

Jesse bit her lip when he opened his mouth wide over her breast, his fangs scraping slightly as he suckled. He was going to bite her with those. She grew so wet at the thought that she slid another inch down his shaft, her body shaking with the need to feel him inside her in every way possible. Fangs, cock, fingers, she wanted it all. She'd had over ten years of foreplay, she was more than ready for the main event.

He paid homage to both her breasts for long moments, seeming to forget his urgency, and she grew restless. She yanked on the long thin braid that framed his face to get his attention, leaning forward to take his ear between her teeth and bite down. Hard. Kit opened his eyes without lifting his mouth from her nipple. "Bite me, Kit. Please, I want you to."

A gritty rumble started in his throat. Jesse watched the whites of his eyes disappear in the blackness, all illusion of humanity gone. She felt him shift position, one arm cradling her hips while the other hand lifted to gently cover her mouth.

She moaned. The others. She'd forgotten the others outside. She kissed and nibbled on his palm, moaning her approval. He was protecting her, but it felt so dirty. So hot. Her thighs tightened around him, silently begging him to finish this. To fuck her.

Kit bit down on her breast, upper and lower fangs piercing the abundant flesh, and she cried out against his hand. The pain lasted only seconds, and then it changed. Something new raced through her bloodstream like a drug. She could feel it as it traveled through her body.

God, had he injected her with some kind of aphrodisiac? She'd already been aroused beyond the point of reason, but this was insanity. Every inch of her flesh was on fire. Everywhere he touched her electricity shot through her body. Little orgasmic explosions, each building on the other until she climaxed from his bite alone.

He lifted his mouth, laving the bloody pierce points, healing them with his saliva. "Great Mother, Jesse. I've never done that before." His voice was so garbled she could barely understand him. "I had no idea I would be able to feel...Oh, yes, angel, yes take me inside you. I can't wait any longer...I need...to... Ahhh."

Jesse had been pushing forward, trying to force him inside her with her hips and thighs. One moment he was still, savoring the sensation, the next he lost all control. He opened his mouth on a silent roar and powered his cock past her resistant flesh, filling her until even in her drugged state she had a hard time believing she could physically take more. There was always more.

"So tight, *sarasvatti.* Fuck, you're squeezing me so tight. So good..." He was muttering as he pounded her hips into the wall, his fingers slipping into her open mouth. She sucked them hard, and he growled. "That's right, angel. Oh, you're good at that aren't you? You want to suck my cock?" She nodded enthusiastically. "It's soaked with your come, your juices. But you wouldn't care, would you? You'd still love it."

Kit licked the traces of her blood off his lips, his gaze ensnared by her sucking mouth. "That may have to stay a dream, Jesse love. Because. I can't. Stop. Fucking you." He pulled his fingers out of her mouth, replacing them with his lips. His arm slid beneath her thigh, lifting it high.

Yes. Jesse felt him spread her wide and change the angle of his thrusts, hitting a spot deep inside her that threw her off the edge of one world and into another. She screamed against his mouth, her spine bowing at the powerful shockwaves jolting her body.

She took his full, lower lip between her teeth, not realizing that she'd broken the skin until he roared. The sound echoed off the cave walls, and he quickened his thrusts. She felt his muscles ripple with the powerful force of his climax. For a moment it seemed that his cock grew larger, pumping her full of his come as he shook against her.

Her glasses were twisted on her face, and so foggy she could barely see. She reached up to take them off and froze with them in her hand. Over Kit's shoulder she could see him standing there.

Max.

Her instinctual fear was replaced by curiosity. He could have hidden in the shadows, could have watched without her knowing that he was there. Had he wanted her to see him there? He studied her in silence for a moment, walking away without a word or sound. Was he spying for his elders? Or was there another reason entirely?

"He wants you."

Kit pulled back in time to see Jesse's jaw drop. He kissed her cheek as she shook her head in denial. "You're wrong. He drugged me. And then, he brought me here for trial. That does not sound like a man with a crush. It sounds like someone who hates me."

"I know my cousin. He does his duty because that is who he is. And he'll stay away because he knows you're mine. But he wants you. That was his way of letting me know."

Kit set her down gently, pulling a towel from the ether to wipe the moisture from her body. Jesse tilted her head. "That doesn't bother you at all?"

He quirked his lips. "I've tasted your blood, taken your virginity and filled you with my seed. I am too satisfied to be upset. Max is closer to me than my own brother. He would never take by force that which is mine. Unless I invited him to share."

"*What?*" She squeaked in laughter as he tickled her ribs, attempting to distract her from his words. But even more than the potential invitation, one phrase stood out to her. "Kit? Um...about that seed thing...?"

He grew somber. "The Mother ensured long ago that my people would never again be able to procreate with a human." Kit curved his large palm low on her belly, and she shivered. "There was true wisdom in her decision, though right at this moment, there is nothing I can think of that would be quite as beautiful as you, pregnant with my child."

A subtle noise alerted them to Elam's presence in the doorway. "Kittim of the Sariel guard. I have been informed that the way has been cleared. Take the human, the Beta and...my son...to the Hall of Records and prepare yourselves for your audience with the Old Ones. When dawn lights the sky, you will all stand before them." The towering man who looked a lot like Max turned to leave as soon as he made the announcement, his face expressionless.

"I have a hard time believing he's Max's father. Brother *maybe*." Jesse was still reeling from the sincerity in his voice when Kit had talked about giving her a child. She had a million questions. Why couldn't his bite change her? Why couldn't they have a baby together? More importantly, what did he mean when he had said "again"? Why could they have children with another species before, but not now?

Kit scooped up the satchel and her bags, flashed their clothes back on with a swiftness that was a little disconcerting, and took her hand. "Believe me, that man is older than the flood. Jesse, I'm going to need you to trust me. You and Dydarren both." He pulled her along behind him, stopping when they reached Max and Jasyn.

Jesse watched the cousins stare at each other in silence. They almost seemed to be communicating without words. Kit spoke softly. "Can I count on you?"

Max glanced quickly at Jesse before meeting Kit's gaze once more. "I give my oath freely."

Jesse and Jasyn looked at the warriors, then at each other with a shrug. "Any clue what they're talking about?"

She smiled at his put-upon tone. "Nope. You?"

Kit jerked her closer to him, glaring at the Were. “We’re talking about getting you two the hell out of here before your sentence can be imposed.”

The Beta flinched, his lip curling in a threatening snarl. “*Our* sentence? What’s my crime? For that matter, what is hers, apart from starring in a few racy dreams?”

Kit looked just as upset. “There is only one reason the two of you would be sent with us to the Hall of Records. The Old Ones do not expect you to leave our settlement alive. Either of you.”

“So, since I’m going to die, do you think I could have my camera? I *have* to get some pictures of this place.” Jesse had an itchy trigger finger again. She didn’t have time for fear. There was too much beauty and grandeur around her. She had to capture it. And she wouldn’t mind getting a few shots of Kit as well.

In the last few days she’d met some of the most exquisite people she’d ever seen in her life. And with her career that was saying something. Kit surpassed them all. He was a mountain of dark bronze man-flesh and muscle. Sculpted and beautifully defined despite his enormous size. And that hair. Dark and long, with two matching, slender braids framing his high cheekbones and strong jaw line. He was every inch the warrior.

But it was his face that made her think of fallen angels and gods. She wasn’t sure why he hadn’t been attacked by more Unborns and Trueblood females, unless he used the same ability she’d seen Max employ on their journey. When she'd first met the guard at Haven, he'd seemed attractive, but not particularly noteworthy. As they came closer to his settlement, he'd let his guard down. She recalled looking as they took turns carrying her, racing through England and into Scotland, and being stunned by his flawless features.

But there was no comparison to Kit's luscious lips and endless lashes. Even the thick scar on his chest was sexy. Years ago, during one of their shared dreams, he'd laughed it off. Calling it the only battle wound that hadn't healed. "The mark of what I am." Now she wondered anew.

"Don't joke about dying, Jesse, please. You're giving the guards a heart attack. They're tightly wound as it is." Jasyn slipped her camera out of the bag dangling from Kit's shoulders, handing it to her with a gallant bow. Her warrior just grunted, his mind on other things.

"Hannah would love this place. She liked to draw. She wanted to travel the world and sketch the pyramids and the temples of Greece. That's why she'd left New York in the first place. Lago Maggiore was one of her first stops. And her last." Jasyn's voice grew soft with memory and longing.

Jesse turned her camera on him, seeing more, as she always did, through the lens. "It's not about Nicolette anymore is it? You think *Hannah* won't take you back." She could see it in his expression. Had he always held her up on that pedestal he had her on now? Was that why he'd waited until it was too late to take her as his mate?

She snapped the picture and lowered the camera, putting her hand on his arm. "You have to trust me on this. She loves you. Plus, from what I've seen over the years, this mate stuff is pretty set in stone right? I mean, a connection like that is unbreakable isn't it? Regardless of how many years you spend arguing with yourself. And now that we know that vampires and werewolves can mate..."

They'd stopped in front of a magnificent structure carved into the rock, but the three men were ignoring the wonder, studying her instead. She shrugged, snapping a quick picture of the epic columns and archway covered with intricate designs and symbols. "What? Do you know how hard we have it as humans? Wandering around without your senses of smell or telepathy. We don't blood bond. We date. We spend most of the time trying to figure out if we can live with his snoring and if he can stand our crazy family at Christmas."

She rolled her eyes. "Every woman I've ever known would kill to know that her man has no doubts, that she belongs to him in a way so elemental, so primal that not even death could part them." She pointed a finger into Jasyn's muscled chest. "I may be a powerless little mortal, but even I know that when you have love, you take it and grab it and don't let it go until they rip it from your cold, dead hands. And when you have a mate, you, well, you mate."

Jesse blushed as they continued staring at her in silence. This is why she worked alone. She had a tendency to say too much. Jasyn started smiling, taking her finger from his chest and gifting the tip with a gentle kiss.

"You sure are bossy for a powerless little mortal." He winked. "But I thank you. Now let's plan our grand escape. I suddenly have an overwhelming desire to get home."

He walked ahead of them, whistling, and Jesse grinned at the two flabbergasted men beside her.

"That was amazing, my lady. Miss Regina has told me how stubborn the Beta can be."

Kit laughed. "You don't know the half of it, Max, my friend. There isn't a Were or Unborn alive who hasn't tried to get through to him. But it was Jesse who finally succeeded. There will be poems and songs about this day."

Jesse shrugged, secretly flattered. "Sometimes it takes a human touch, I guess." They started up the large steps and into the building, but Jesse hesitated. "Kit?"

He stopped, turning to hide her from Max's view. "What is it?"

She looked down at her camera, unwilling to meet his gaze. "Do your people have mates?"

He lifted her chin, caressing her lower lip with his thumb. His sad smile sent a sharp pain through her heart. "No, *sarasvatti*. Our creator never gifted us with that blessing. Love was not the reason we were made."

Kit herded her up the stairs, waiting until they were safely inside before bending to kiss her gently. "But that doesn't mean we *can't* love, Jesse. Just as fiercely as any Trueblood loves his *grathita.*"

Jesse followed him inside, wishing with all her heart his words were true.

Chapter Five

He hadn't been inside these halls for hundreds of years. In truth, close to two thousand had passed. He recalled it clearly. The day Elam and Kit's father had brought him to the Halls of Record for the first time. The night was branded on his heart. It was the night he had truly understood who his mother was. And the last time he had seen his father.

Kit could see the awe on Jesse's face as she clicked away with her camera like a wild thing. She did love to take pictures. Max would confiscate it before she left, of course, but he didn't see any harm in putting her at ease for now.

He had a flash of memory. She was eleven, and she'd told him she was going to be a photographer because she wanted the power to stop time like he did. He hadn't realized then what she could do, that Jesse was a real girl who'd somehow made a connection with him. A connection that showed her a world she should have never known, a world far too dangerous for a human to comprehend.

When Max had told him that she'd "dreamt" through his eyes, that she'd experienced things with him when he hadn't had any awareness of her in his mind, the thought of such an invasion threw him. But he couldn't find the anger the situation would seem to call for. She was his angel. He knew her soul as well as he knew his own. She would never betray him.

All those moments that he had walked, hidden in shadow among the humans, longing for one moment for her to be real...she'd been there. She *saw* him. And if this night was all they could have, it would be enough.

He looked around the cavernous construct, trying to see it through her eyes. His people had always been artisans, amazingly skilled with molding stone to their will. Before they found roots here, they'd left evidence of their love for building throughout the ancient world. But none of those works could compare with this place.

There were twelve inner columns, four in every room, each made of jewels found deep beneath the ground. The emeralds, rubies and diamonds had all been polished and shaped by loving hands.

The rock floor had been polished to a black, mirror-like shine. It was interrupted by carvings of labyrinthine shapes filled with silver, gold, and copper, each one leading the way to a corresponding hall.

Max came up beside him. "You told me, my cousin, but I didn't believe. It is truly magnificent."

"Wait. Are you telling me that you've never been in here before? But it's right here. In the center of your settlement. A couple of flights of stairs away." Jesse's voice was getting progressively higher with disbelief.

Kit laid a hand on her shoulder. "Humans have parks and cathedrals next to their homes that they never explore. Truebloods and Weres live among them, but they never notice. It's no different for us."

She furrowed her brow in a grumpy glare. "You have a point. But we don't have anything like this. Did Max's father call it the Halls of Record? Is it like a library? Where are the books?"

Kit looked at Max, whose lips were tilted in charmed bemusement. "She talks a lot."

Kit nodded, feeling lighter than he had in decades. "That she does, cousin. But a good spanking usually does the trick. Drives her so crazy she can't think of anything but the need to come."

He watched her face turn the same shade as her hair. She chewed on her upper lip, fingers turning white as she clutched her camera. He would have apologized for embarrassing her if he didn't scent her arousal, rich and sweet, in the air.

He saw the moment she realized that every man in the room had the ability to sense her desire. "Great." She muttered to herself for a few minutes, and Kit decided to change the subject before she tried to melt into the floor.

"The Halls of Record *is* a library, of sorts. It was one of the first places our elders built when they decided to settle here. It was meant to store the knowledge of our people, to ensure that those called to serve would never forget where they came from, or why they had chosen to live as they did."

He walked along the copper line, the sound of his steps reverberating off the walls. "This cord leads to the hall of water. The glory of our beginnings and a record of our finest accomplishments are written on those walls."

His long legs took a wide step, leading him to the line of gold. "This cord leads to the hall of fire. Where, in passion and violence, our bridges were burned. The stories told on these walls are not for the faint of heart." Kit wondered what she would think when she saw what his people had done. Would she look at him differently?

"And the silver cord?" Jesse's compassionate voice reached out and wrapped around him. Warmed him.

"That leads to the hall of air. Of possibilities and promise. It shows when we were saved, when we were taken in by the old Sariel Mediator, and chose to live a life dedicated to service."

"Looks like we were expected." Everyone turned to see Jasyn at the opening to the hall of water. "We have bedrolls and enough food to feed a village in there." He waggled his eyebrows at Jesse. "Wanna frolic in the waterfall?"

"Waterfall?" Jesse jogged over to the entrance, gasping as she peered inside. "Oh my God there's a waterfall in here. How did they do that?"

She turned to Kit, her smile radiant. "I could *shower*. Oh wait, can I? Is it a sacred waterfall or something?" She snapped a picture, heading deeper into the room before he could respond.

"Should we keep the Beta in the main entryway? If we allow him access to all our knowledge, he could share it with the others once he escapes."

Kit shrugged. "I don't see why we should. Times are changing, Max. I know you see it too. Why shouldn't we learn from the Truebloods and Weres, and shed some light into *our* dark corners?"

Max considered his words in silence for a moment, his voice hushed with anger when he finally spoke. "My father believes the choosing has been compromised."

Kit wasn't surprised. "I know. It is just my mother, cleaning up after her first mistake." He shook his head at Max's questioning look. "It doesn't matter, cousin. I resigned myself to this fate a long time ago."

Jesse laughed, and both men turned toward the sound like moths to a flame. "Or I thought I had. Until today."

Her digital camera had died. She longed for her old standby, but she'd left that at home. Truth be told, she didn't believe that a still image could capture what she was seeing. Which was hard for the photographer in her to admit. But there was just too much to take in. Too much beauty...and horror.

The artwork on the walls so far surpassed anything Jesse had ever seen that it was difficult to process. The painted plants and creatures seemed to breathe with life.

She reached out to touch the wall, sure she would feel the rough texture of the tree bark beneath her palm. More than realistic, as she stared, the art began to pull her in, sharing the smells, sounds, and emotions of the story it told.

She was in a forest. Trees that soared to the heavens, far beyond the high ceiling of the hall. Jesse could feel the gods smiling down on their creations. The wonders they had made pleased them greatly.

For a while.

Two of the younger gods, brothers who were competitive in nature, began to create new life for sport. Strange animals and murderous plants began appearing all around the peaceful Eden, each one more unusual, more grotesque than the last. The older gods stepped in, demanding boundaries. They would hold a contest.

They would each be allowed to create seven new life forms. For seven days those life forms would be allowed to exist in the newly created world, and the gods would observe. At the end of those allotted days, the gods would pick a winner, and that creation alone would be allowed to remain.

The brothers dove into the competition with gusto. But a pattern soon began to emerge. The younger brother was continuously praised for his creations by the other gods, for he made the most beautiful and magical of creatures, though most lacked the will to conquer adversity. The elder's creations, on the other hand, made his peers uncomfortable, nervous. They were twisted and dark, and always prone to violence.

The eldest grew envious, deciding that he had to win, regardless of the cost. Sneaking into his brother's workshop, he noticed a project that had been discarded before it could be completed. It was a being whose form and features were identical to the gods themselves. It was a work of art. Or it would be, when he was done with it.

He sent his finished product out into the world to be judged, discovering a flaw he had missed in his tinkering. The giant god-beast he had fashioned was *not* destroying his younger brother's creations the way he had imagined. Instead, it was building itself a magnificent shelter, studying the stars and creating intricate tools to carve stone replicas of the other creatures that passed by.

The god was angered. He had stolen a piece of the Soul Seed from the Mother's womb to bring this being to life. Gifted it with physical and mental superiority, heightened instincts and intimidating size, but the life form was not cooperating. He'd taken the ultimate leap, and he'd failed.

Then something happened.

The other gods, particularly the Great Mother and Father, were fascinated. So enamored at this being that they were not angered at how it was created. So entranced that they asked the eldest brother to make more, that they might watch how the creature interacted with its own kind. Even his younger brother shared in the joy, helping him by forming more beings.

The Mother named them Watchers, Igigi. The guardians of all they surveyed, all the other creatures. The Igigi, with their godlike intelligence and curiosity, advanced faster than any of the other beings of the earth. They tilled the land for farming, built great temples climbing to the heavens and ruled over the lesser beasts.

Things came easily to them, too easily. Without any rules to guide them, their reverence for the gods soon disappeared, as did their respect for the animals that roamed the land beside them. They became arrogant, and their dissatisfaction grew.

Jesse sensed a change, a darker thread appearing in the narrative on the wall. The god who had created the first of the Igigi had been whispering in their dreams, telling them of the pantheon of gods who watched them for amusement, allowing them to do all the manual labor, never sharing the riches of heaven.

When the Great Mother announced that she had decided to create a more fragile being, made in the image of the gods but without their more obvious powers, the god scoffed.

But the others bowed to the Mother's brilliance, their energies now focused on preparing the way, and protecting the small mortals.

Lost in his cups one eve, the younger brother admitted to the Igigi's god that these creatures, these humans, were all the more special for their vulnerability. And something else. They'd been blessed with the one thing no other creature had received before. Not only a piece of the Soul Seed, but also the Light from the Great Mother's own heart. A gift the other gods had coveted since time began.

The elder's rage knew no bounds. He had plans for the Igigi, plans to overtake heaven and Earth and rule in the Father's stead. Plans that did *not* include these new creations, these humans blessed with the Mother's Light.

He declared war. But when he called his Igigi to fight, only half of them followed. The others resisted the mindless slaughter of beings that they were more inclined to protect...beings more like them than not.

The fight was bloody and devastating, but short lived. The other gods were simply too strong, and too determined to protect the humans. In a fit of rage, the god of the Igigi decided to destroy everything on the earth, including his own failed experiment. For if his powerful giants could not wipe the humans from existence, how would they help him defeat the Mother and her minions?

He opened the heavens and torrents of rain fell from the sky. No matter how the others pleaded, he would not stop the deluge. He knew the Great Mother would never stop him outright, she could not interfere directly with another god.

But his younger brother was clever. He revealed himself to a small community of humans, as well as the Igigi who had resisted his brother's violent request, and encouraged them to work together in secret to survive.

The Igigi were inventive and swift, creating a barge as big as a city made of the sturdiest trees in the forest. They saved as many animals and humans as they could, and waited out the angry god.

"You've got to be kidding me."

"Sounds familiar, doesn't it?"

Jesse pulled her hand from the wall and whirled around, her forehead bumping into the solid wall of Kit's chest. He cupped her shoulders gently, his thumbs caressing her collarbone as she steadied herself. "A little. So, are we talking Noah's Ark here?"

Kit shrugged. "Gilgamesh, Noah, the story has been around as long as there have been humans to tell it. It's changed over the years, but the flood itself was too powerful, too profound a memory to fully fade into oblivion."

Jesse had been so wrapped up in the story she hadn't realized she'd moved into the hall of fire. "So, what happened to the god who started the flood?"

"Our creator, who made us out of stolen bits and a large dash of his own ego?" Kit sneered at the god's image on the wall. "He was contained. The rain stopped and those who remained began building again, having children, surviving. Our people mingled with the human race, though *they* never quite got over their fear of our power and size."

He slid his hands off her shoulders, his fingers curling, white knuckled as he eyed the last image in the hall of fire. "It ate at him, that we'd been allowed to survive. That he'd been scolded for what he saw as *our* weakness. He demanded that we be erased from existence. That it was his right as our creator to make that decision."

Jesse followed the image as it began to lighten, to form the beautiful shape of light that she knew was the goddess of the vampires and werewolves. "The Mother?"

He lowered his head in acknowledgment. "Rightly or wrongly, she denied him. Protecting us, as much as she could, from direct punishment. We held the Soul Seed within us, and she believed we should be allowed to evolve. She even gave us the ability to walk unseen through the world. We call it shadow stalking. But we were so damned arrogant, and even though he'd been restrained, he was a god. We gave him ample ammunition, and he began to use his abilities on more fertile minds. Human minds that didn't have the strength to resist a god.

"He showed himself to their leaders, demanded worship and stoked their fears. He became their storm god, and his hatred for the Igigi gave them permission to hate us as well."

Jesse studied the depiction of that time. Kit's people were chained and whipped, run out of town by torch carrying mobs, or forced into service.

Her expression must have revealed her horror, because he reached out to take her hand. "No, *sarasvatti*, do not pity us. We made his work easy. We were stronger, faster and bigger than any other creature on the planet, and we knew it. The Igigi were gluttonous and lazy, prone to violence and filled with avarice. We deserved everything we got.

But even those of us who attempted to adapt to human civilization were met with scorn and ridicule. And lo to any of our kind who dared fall in love with a human woman." Jesse bit her lip in silent pain as he squeezed her fingers in unconscious distress. "Be glad we do not live in those times, my angel. What they did to the women who loved us, to our offspring, was far worse than anything that could be done to us."

He talked like he'd seen it firsthand. Jesse's concern overrode her curiosity. He was in pain. She could feel it. She pulled him toward the entryway of the final hall, away from the terrible images of the past. "It was wrong. No matter how bad you think *you* were, they were wrong to treat you that way. But your kind doesn't have the monopoly on bad character traits. Humans are capable of horrible things in the name of fear and jealousy. You would think the gods could have created a less flawed creature."

Kit's expression softened. "You're missing the point, Jesse. Your flaws are what make you so special. The children of the gods, the Igigi, even the Vampire and Were species...they were given abilities to ensure their superiority. Abilities like longevity, superhuman strength, the ability to change their forms.

"Yet, despite your short life spans and physical inferiority, humans are the ruling species on the planet. You have a burning desire within you to survive, to learn and grow. You have the Mother's Light inside you, filling you with compassion and determination.

"We have millennia to wander this world. You have a moment in time." He smiled. "And what wonders I've seen you do with that single moment."

"Finish the story." The admiration in his voice was making her uncomfortable. What had she done with her moment? Besides hiding behind her camera, watching other people's mistakes, other people's bravery, and dreaming of someone else's adventures.

Kit had saved thousands of lives, defended the Sariels loyally and faithfully. He acted like none of his sacrifices mattered.

"There isn't much more to tell, *sarasvatti.* The few anomalous creatures, other than the Igigi, who had survived the flood were destroyed by the protectors the Great Mother had created to watch over the humans."

She nodded, knowing this part from her visions. The Weres and Vampires were supposed to guide and guard the humans from the dangers of the world. It hadn't taken long for them to resent their task, wanting to rule instead. They started killing each other and any humans that got in their way, until their goddess abandoned them and gave a few select females the ability to destroy them from within. Readers like Regina.

"The Mother offered us her protection once more, this time taking away our ability to procreate with humans so that no other child would suffer what those few hybrids had to go through. We spread out, small families and factions going to the far reaches of the earth, surviving as best we could. One by one the others were lost. They gave in to violence and vice and disappeared. Finally, a day came when we realized that we were all that was left of our species. And that something had to change."

He pointed to the image of a giant signing a scroll in blood beside a handsome blond vampire. "When the Great War between the Shadow Wolves and Truebloods occurred, we tried to remain on the sidelines, but the shamans of the Shadow Wolves wanted to study us, to find a way to combine our obvious size and strength with their black magic and shifting capabilities. A few atrocities were created from our captured brethren, and that's when my father knew we had to join forces with the Truebloods. Not long after, the Mediator's brother saved his life in battle, and my father vowed the service and fealty of all our people to his clan. We were given a purpose. We became the Sariel guard."

There was something he wasn't telling her, she could feel it. Jesse wanted to ask him about the rest of the pictures on the walls. About the pale, opalescent stone gracing the pedestal in the middle of the hall. She wanted to find out how long he'd lived, to ask him why he hadn't really questioned her ability to gain access to his mind. Most importantly, she wanted to know why his dark eyes held so much resignation. Such loneliness.

She wanted to know, but she'd barely gotten the chance to open her mouth before he was covering it with his own. Kit was obviously done talking. He ate at her mouth with a desperation she couldn't help but respond to.

He lifted her like a babe in his arms, carrying her back, she knew, toward the hall of water. She dragged her lips away, noticing Jasyn standing shirtless in the main entranceway. He was a truly beautiful Were, his smile bittersweet as he nodded respectfully toward Kit when he stopped beside him.

"I'll be outside, taking the next watch for a few hours. Don't worry, I know how to keep out of sight when I'm not wanted." His gaze skimmed Jesse's face, and she realized he was thinking of Hannah again. She lifted her hand from Kit's shoulder and reached out to him, but Jasyn took a step back, out of reach. He winked. "I have a sudden longing to howl at the moon."

The air around him shimmered, and he began to shift. She gasped, and Kit bit her earlobe. "Watch."

As if she could take her eyes away. She'd seen Weres shift before, but only in dreams and visions. She knew Weres could take two shapes other than their human form, resembling either an overly large timber wolf, or a monstrous human-wolf hybrid. But just like everything else, her knowledge was all theory and no practice. So she watched.

Jasyn's muscles and bones were shifting and rippling, his body curled in momentary agony as he changed. Black hair sprouted from his face and arms, hiding his masculine features under a silky pelt.

She saw the monster, her human heart fluttering in instinctive, momentary fear when his light, canine eyes turned her way. This was Jasyn, she reminded herself. She forced a grin, and he curled his lips back, baring his fangs in a relieved smile.

In seconds the transformation was complete, and he was loping away on four paws, a beautiful ebony wolf. "Wow."

"Don't be too impressed. That pup has a giant-sized ego already. Just like his brother." Kit nuzzled her neck and started walking again. "*You* have too many clothes on."

Jesse felt a cool breeze along her thigh, and her mouth went dry. "I guess you solved that problem. Where are you taking me?"

Kit's answer was another kiss, tempting her mouth open with his tongue. Jesse melted against him. God, his taste was addictive. She closed her lips around his tongue and sucked hard, imagining it was his cock in her mouth, thrusting in and out as she swallowed him as deep as he could go.

His broken groan vibrated against her chest, telling her he was thinking the same thing she was. She felt his fangs extend with his arousal, the sharp edges pressing against her lips. Desire slammed into her like a tsunami, demanding release. She wanted him inside her. Filling her. Wanted to experience everything. With Kit.

Jesse wrapped her arms around his neck and twisted until her legs were clinging to his hips. Kit growled, stumbling at the feel of her bare, soaking sex against him. "*Jesse.* Angel, slow down, you're driving me crazy."

"No. I want you now. Please, Kit. Bite me again." She rubbed her heavy breasts against his nipples teasingly, drawing his gaze to the marks he'd left behind the last time she'd been in his arms.

"No? Your impatience is going to get you in trouble, *sarasvatti.*" His rough warning belied the tenderness he used as he pulled off her glasses and set them carefully on a nearby ledge. He didn't take his gaze from hers as he stepped beneath the surprisingly warm waterfall. His expression made her shiver.

Kit set her on a smooth stone seat beneath the watery spray, pulling her hair out of its loose bun and spreading it over her shoulders. "I think I've told you before, it's a sin against the gods to hide such beauty from the world. Your hair rivals the flame of the setting sun."

He wrapped her long, wet curls around his fist, pulling her head back to meet his gaze. "Do you trust me, angel?"

There was no hesitation. "Yes."

"That's good. That's good because I'm not sure *I* trust me, not when it comes to you. I have to remind myself that you're human, fragile. Have to resist my instincts to take you as hard and deep as I'm dying to. To do all that I want to do to you. With you."

Her clit was throbbing at his words. "Don't. Don't hold back, please. I trust you. I can take anything you can dish out. I *want* it."

Kit's lips tilted in that sexy almost-smile that drove her crazy. "I was hoping you'd say that. Max? I think my Jesse just invited you inside."

Chapter Six

Max? Jesse felt her jaw drop, covering her breasts with her hands as she squinted across the room. He was there, standing so still she couldn't tell if he was breathing. "Kit?"

Kit knelt in the pool at her feet, but she still had to tilt her head to meet his gaze. "I trust Max with my life. More importantly, I trust him with yours." His features tightened with lust and something else. Concern.

"I've asked him to watch over you when I can't. It is not a simple request, given our code, his position with the guard."

Jesse bit her lip. "I'm confused. Is he going to...are we all...?"

"No, *sarasvatti.* You are mine. I'm not sure I could share you with anyone. Max knows that. It is an old tradition of my people. When a warrior goes into a battle he may not survive, he chooses a proxy, a guardian whom he trusts to protect what he cherishes the most. I want Max to watch you take your pleasure. I want him to see how beautiful you are, how special. He needs to understand how important you are to me, so that he will protect you when I no longer can."

She could hear the sincerity in his voice. The intensity. She flicked a nervous glance toward Kit's cousin. He was staring at his feet, unmoving. Waiting for her to decide.

It struck her how many times she'd been in Max's position. Watching from a distance as other people reveled in their passions. She was embarrassed to admit how often she'd been aroused as she snapped her illicit photographs, how exciting it was to be the observer.

How much more exciting would it be to be knowingly observed?

Jesse blushed, her thighs tingling at the thought. Max inhaled sharply, his head jerking up as he finally looked her way. He knew. She kept forgetting about their heightened senses.

"I told you she was unique, didn't I, Maximus? So innocent and yet so openly sensual." He ran the backs of his knuckles along the tops of her breasts lightly. "As irresistible as Eve herself."

He lifted her trembling hands from her breasts, kissing each palm in turn. "Let him see you, angel. See the perfection I thought I'd only dreamt of all these years."

A sound emerged from Max's chest that drew Jesse's gaze. Kit's fingers were caressing her, her arms, her breasts, her legs. And Max was watching every move in silence, his desire plain for her to see.

Something came over her. Jesse knew she should be covering herself, demanding that Kit return her clothes or make Max leave. But she didn't. She lifted her chin and arched her back, wantonly displaying her breasts for both men to see.

"You are such a bad girl, *sarasvatti.*" Kit's words were soft and harsh against the base of her neck before he scraped her sensitive skin with his fangs. He rolled one of her nipples between his forefinger and thumb, causing her to gasp and shift on the damp rock beneath her.

He raised his voice, including Max in their conversation once more. "Her body responds so beautifully to my touch. Show him, angel. Show him how wet you are already. For me."

His hand slid from her breast to her thigh, pressing gently, letting her know what he wanted her to do. Jesse spread her legs, unable to stop the whimper of desire that escaped her lips.

Kit slipped two of his fingers inside her aching sex, soaking them with her juices. He pulled them out, ignoring her protesting moan, to suck them into his mouth, his eyes closing at the taste. "So delicious. I've never tasted anything so sweet. I need more."

He buried his face between her thighs with a feral growl. Jesse leaned against the rocks, holding on to his head as the water pulsed against her. He was fucking her with his tongue, his fingers spreading her thighs wide and high, holding her open for him.

Max is watching. Oh God, Max is watching. It was repeating over and over in her brain like a mantra. Her body was on fire for Kit, loving what he was doing, craving it. But the knowledge that he was doing it for an audience sharpened every sensation, heightening her pleasure.

She tried to focus on Max, and realized he'd moved closer. And his shirt had disappeared. He was thicker, beefier than Kit, but his chest bore the same large scar as his cousin's. And his eyes held the same dark intensity.

He didn't leer or wink disrespectfully, nor did he smile in a harmless, reassuring way. His expression was one of...wonder. He was looking at her body as though he'd never seen anything more beautiful. No one but Kit had ever looked at her like that. She was too tall, too broad shouldered, and usually far too big for the average human male.

But not for the average giant. That thought was the ultimate aphrodisiac.

Kit was devastating her with his tongue, his teeth. With his thick, knowing fingers. Her vision blurred and her body bowed in response. She gripped his head in her hands, lifting her hips up to meet his mouth. "Kit. *Yes.* Don't stop. Please, don't stop."

His fingers tightened on her thighs, and he lifted his mouth. "My greedy angel. Come for me, Jesse. Come against my tongue. I want it all. Every fucking drop."

"*Kit.*" He swirled his tongue deep inside her, his thumb pressing her aching clit, and Jesse couldn't hold back. She cried out with the power of her climax, coming against his mouth while the water poured down her burning skin. Kit pulled her closer, groaning with approval as his raspy tongue lapped at the lips of her sex, as if he couldn't get enough of her taste.

Her mouth opened on a soundless scream when his fangs pierced her inner thigh. Fire flowed through her veins and into her core from the drugging ecstasy of his bite.

Jesse felt herself coming again and again, waves of pleasure that seemed to grow stronger with every moment that passed. Her gaze was captured by a snarling Max, his own fangs extended while his attention fixated on the healing mark on her breast. She closed her eyes, her body on overload.

"I can't...it's too much."

Kit cleaned the wound with his tongue before getting up to stand beside her. Her heavy lids lifted to see his massive cock hovering just out of reach. She wanted to taste it, to return the pleasure he'd given her, but he didn't give her the chance. "It's not enough, *sarasvatti*. It will never be enough. I need to be inside you."

He lifted her by her hips, sliding beneath her so she was sitting on his lap. Kit leaned his chin on her shoulder, holding her while she rubbed against him, her body screaming for his. "Now you know."

Max answered, his voice rough with longing in the large hall. "Now I know."

"I will have your vow."

Jesse watched Max kneel on the marbled floor in front of them. “With the blood I spill, you have my vow. Only death can break it.” He pulled a dagger from his boot, slicing open his palm before Jesse could stop him.

“What are you doing?”

Kit pulled her back against his chest, his hands tightening on her hips as he probed her with his cock. “*We* are protecting you, *sarasvatti.* And I? I am loving you.” The last words were whispered softly in her ear before he pulled her down, filling her heated sex with his thick erection.

Her body was still reacting from his bite, fluttering with residual contractions as he stretched her. A part of her seemed to watch from the corner of the room in disbelief. She watched as the voluptuous goddess threw back her head, her fiery tresses spilling across the bronze giant’s chest as she fought to accept all of him inside her.

She was heedless of the man at their feet. She took his worship as her due while his blood dripped from his clenched fist onto the floor, his other hand cupping his stiff erection through his pants, desperate for his own release.

The woman beneath the waterfall lifted her breasts in her hands, squeezing her nipples hard between her fingers, loving the sharp sensation. She was shameless in her sensuality. Focused only on the pleasure hammering her body as her lover drove her down onto his cock, faster and deeper with every stroke.

She came back to herself with a cry as Kit lifted one hand from her hips to spank her clit. "That's what I want. I want to hear your cries of need echoing through these somber halls."

He spanked her again, growling when she tightened her muscles around him in response. "You're like hot silk around my cock. Your pussy grips me tighter than any fist, *sarasvatti.* Great Mother, *Jesse*, I've never felt such heat."

Jesse freed her breasts, reaching back to grip his thighs for balance as she rode him harder, forcing him in as deep as he could go. Kit gave a shout of surprised pleasure. "*Yes.* That's it, angel. Take what is yours. Fuck me."

She rocked against him, reveling in the stretch, the sting as her internal muscles were forced to give way to his hard shaft. His mouth opened on her shoulder, fangs pressing against her flesh but not breaking the skin. She could feel his restraint, feel him holding back, maintaining his control. But she didn't want him to have control. Not now.

Jesse's nails dug sharply into his thighs and she lifted herself up, until the head of his cock was barely inside her, and stopped. She clenched her muscles rhythmically around the tip of his shaft, but held herself back, keeping what he wanted just out of reach.

Kit's grip tightened on her hips. "Jesse? Baby, you're killing me." She resisted his gentle tug, shaking her head.

Max stilled, tilting his head as he waited to see what she was up to. But Kit knew. "You *think* you want me to lose all my control, *sarasvatti*, but you don't. Or are you angling for a special kind of punishment?"

Jesse shivered at his words, her head filling with images of his style of retribution. Bent over his lap while his hand spanked her until her cheeks were red with the sting. Kneeling at his feet with her hands tied behind her back while he teased her lips with his cock. "Oh God."

"Oh how you tempt me, my angel. But I can't wait anymore. Not another second." He sank his fangs into her neck, drinking her in while the drugging effect of his bite took hold. One bite had been enough to make her near mindless with need. Two threw her completely over the edge.

Starbursts filled her vision and she screamed his name as he stood, still inside her. Her feet dangled, and she was held upright by nothing more than his hands on her waist and his suckling mouth at her neck. She raised her arm to wrap it around his neck, gripping his long hair as he powered into her from behind.

She felt impaled, utterly possessed. Taken. And yet, the strange energy running through her body gave her a sense of power she'd never experienced before. She could feel the electricity of it just under her skin, different from the effects of his last bite, different from the strength of her climax. Jesse started to reach for it, but it disappeared in another wave of pleasure as she sensed Kit coming inside her.

He licked her neck and shoulder tenderly, his hot breath sending shivers across her overly-sensitive skin. "*Sarasvatti.* My gift."

Through her lashes Jesse watched as Max stood, fully clothed once more. His sharp cheekbones were flushed dark with repressed desire as he met her gaze. He dipped his chin, a study in respectful restraint, before he turned to exit the hall, leaving them alone beneath the waterfall.

Kit set her down gently, turning her in his arms to place a tender kiss on her lips. She wobbled a bit, her body still abuzz with sensation. "Easy, angel. Let me take care of you. Just this one last time."

She knew there was something wrong with that statement. Knew that she should question him, but she couldn't fight past the sensual lethargy that weighted her down. She was floating through the air for a moment, and then snuggled into the softest blankets she'd ever felt against her skin.

His lips smoothed over her forehead, her cheeks, her chin, and she curled her body around his heat like a sated cat. "I don't want to wake up yet."

Kit sighed. "Neither do I, Jesse. Neither do I."

"I have to admit that I've imagined you naked once or twice, but I swear, *those two* have never crossed my mind."

Jesse spun around, gasping when she realized she was standing, stark naked in front of Jasyn Dydarren, with Kit and Max sleeping deeply on the cots beside her.

She grabbed the nearest blanket and wrapped it around her body protectively.

She looked around in confusion. They were in the Halls of Record, in the exact place she'd fallen asleep, but something was different. "I'm dreaming."

Jasyn crossed his arms over his chest. "I thought I was the one dreaming. Although if I was, you wouldn't be covered, and we definitely wouldn't be here. My brother told me about this dreamwalking business. Lux and Regina do it all the time, apparently. Personally, I'm not seeing the allure. I'd much rather go back to my usual dreams. Running free through the woods, coming upon a bevy of naked—" He stopped when he caught her irritated gaze. "I'll tell you about it later."

Jesse bit her lip in confusion, looking down at her peaceful giant. He snored. Not *giant* snoring. Just a little. The fact that she thought it was sexy said something about her state of mind. She rolled her eyes. "In all my dreams, we've either been together, or I've experienced things through him. Why is he still sleeping?"

"Because this isn't his dream, little one."

Jesse's heart jumped to her throat. "Mom?"

Her mother was just as petite and beautiful as she remembered, her dark mahogany hair falling softly against her sundress, her eyes radiant. She was standing in the entrance of the hall of water, smiling in the mischievous way she always did when she had a secret.

Jasyn stood straighter, dropping his arms awkwardly before reaching out to shake the new arrival's hand. "Yep.

Definitely not my dream. I never dream of mothers. No offense, ma'am. It's kind of a personal code."

She chuckled, shaking the Were's hand warmly. "I'm so glad I got to meet you, Jasyn Dydarren. I've been rooting for you and that sweet Hannah for years." She waggled her finger at him. "Don't let me down."

"Rooting for them? You've never even met them before."

Her mother shrugged at Jesse's words. "That doesn't mean I haven't been keeping tabs." She raised one thin, strawberry colored eyebrow in Jesse's direction. "It isn't as if you've given me anything exciting to watch. Until recently, that is."

"Great. You're saying we're your soap opera? He isn't a brooding hero in a serial, Mom."

"Don't be silly, dear. Of course he isn't. He *is* just as stubborn as they are though. And definitely brooding. Although he seems much lighter now. I think this trip has been good for him. Maybe he'll actually get off his furry butt and make that girl his mate."

Jasyn barked out a surprised laugh, giving her hand an affectionate squeeze. "I can't argue with both you and your daughter now can I? I promise, the second I escape this gargantuan mausoleum, I'll try to keep the brooding stubbornness to a minimum and make you proud."

He walked over to Jesse, his expression sobering. "Speaking of which, I better get going. I have my marching orders, and a debt to repay."

Jesse wrinkled her brow, perplexed to find him carrying her camera bag, and another satchel that looked stretched to capacity. "Where are you going with that?"

"I'm keeping it safe for you. Stay close to Max and Kit, Jesse. Don't let anyone separate you. If all goes well, I'll see you soon." He popped out of view before she could blink.

"What the hell is going on?"

"Mind your tongue, young lady. Come, there isn't much time." Jesse allowed her mother to pull her through the cavernous rooms, into the hall of air.

"Where is the stone?" The pearl-like stone that had graced the marble pedestal in the center of the room was gone.

Her mother walked over to the far wall, nodding in approval. "I'm glad they left this wall bare. Leaves room for new beginnings. Although it's not the kind of move I'd expect from the Igigi. They are just like the Truebloods and Weres in that way, not exactly open to change." She shrugged. "But then neither are you or your brother. The fact that it took you so long to come and find Kit sort of proves my point.

"That was no ordinary stone, my love. Jasyn Dydarren took it with him for safekeeping. He risks much for his friend. And for you. I really hope he doesn't screw it up with Hannah again. Now there's a girl who deserves a happy ending."

Jesse rubbed her temples. She'd like to think this was just a side effect of her troubled subconscious, but somehow she knew this was no dream. That meant she was really talking to her mother, her deceased mother, who appeared to be matchmaking from the great beyond. "Can we talk about Jasyn's love life later, Mom? I need to know why you're here. My dreams are supposed to be real but...but I saw you..."

"Die? You can say it, honey. It's not a bad word." She smiled. "I love that about you. How curious you always are. Always searching. You're so like your father." Jesse shook her head. Her mother hadn't changed one bit.

"Of course I haven't changed. And I never will." She ignored her daughter's look of surprise and wrapped her arms around her. "I wish I could help you, Jesse. Wish I could make this next part easier."

"What are you talking about?"

"I have to tell you before I go. You're special. You always have been. Remember that, and stay strong."

Jesse gripped her mother's shoulders, feeling a little frantic. "Mom, please don't leave. Why did Jasyn take the stone? Stay and talk to me. What is the next part? What's going to happen?"

"A sacrifice. And there's nothing and no one on Earth that can stop it."

Her mother faded from view, and Jesse choked back a sob. She hadn't realized how much she still missed her until this moment. Sure, her mother was flighty and romantic, a dreamer who drove Jesse and her brother crazy with worry. But she'd been the heart of their small family. And without her, Jesse had been lost.

She looked around the hall, a glimmer of light drawing her gaze to the blank wall. It had been bare moments ago, but now, as she watched, an image was beginning to appear. Fully formed, as though it had been hidden beneath the rock, the vision made Jesse stumble.

"No. No, that can't be true."

Was this why she'd been drawn to come here? Why she felt so strongly that Kit needed her? She'd been thrown for a loop since she'd seen him standing in front of her, real and alive. She hadn't given herself time to wonder why they'd been sent here for the night, why she hadn't been allowed to see any of his people. She hadn't stopped to make him explain.

And from what she was seeing in this painting, she should have. Maybe then she would understand what the violence in the scene meant. Then Kit could laugh and tell her it wasn't what it looked like at all. That he wasn't going to allow himself to be subjected to the future splashed upon the wall.

She traced the image of his face, wracked with indescribable agony and suffering, and knew. She'd loved him all of her life. He'd been her protector, her friend and her fantasy.

Was it only days ago that she had wondered if the reality of her giant would disappoint? She'd been so foolish. With every moment that passed she loved him more. And now what? Was she supposed to just let this future come to pass? Just stand by and allow him to take this path?

A glint of red caught her eye. A woman stood in the final image, her auburn hair flowing down her back, her expression one of disbelief and horror. She was reaching for something, but Jesse couldn't see what it was, it was just outside of the picture. Was it something to save them? She could only hope.

She turned away from the image of Kit collapsing beside the other fallen bodies, all of them as familiar to her as her own. Whatever came next, Jesse was only sure of one thing.

This couldn't happen. She just had to figure out a way to stop it, regardless of what her mother had said. But first she had to wake up.

Chapter Seven

He didn't understand her. Kit found himself wishing he'd had a chance to talk to Lux or Zander. Surely they had both experienced the confusing ways of their *grathitas* enough to have a better idea of how to handle it.

Not for the first time, he felt envy. Jesse had been right. Weres and Vampires had it so much easier. After they bonded, they knew instantly what their significant others were thinking and feeling at all times. His people had been fashioned, not by a loving goddess, but a vengeful male god who had no thought of love, no understanding of the female heart. It was a crippling disadvantage.

When he'd woken before dawn with her in his arms, she'd been restless. Was she dreaming without him then? It made him wonder if, after he was gone, would he be able to visit her in dreams? If so, he wouldn't have a single regret about what was coming.

Kit had woken her with his kiss, loving the quiet intimacy of the moment, imagining a life of mornings waking beside her. At first she responded, her sensual nature unable to resist the soft caress. But in seconds she was pushing him away, scrambling backward on the cot, her blanket clutched to her chest.

She'd apologized, but it hadn't made her any less skittish. When she grabbed her pile of clothes and mumbled something about changing in private, he'd decided to give her some space.

This was new to him. He'd watched her grow up, knew how she responded to his touch, knew every line and curve on her expressive face. But this woman in front of him, her smell, her insight, her courage...this woman was different. Harder to predict.

He loved her. Far more than he'd believed a being of his age and experience could. She made him feel young and reckless. The mere thought of her made him hard as granite. He wanted to spend the next thousand years exploring her body, bringing her pleasure and keeping her safe.

Damn the Fates. The only way he could keep her safe now was to be the unflinching warrior, the Sariel guard that he was, one more time. He would have to send her away. He would have to fulfill his obligation to his people. Do his duty.

"Kittim. Join us. *Now.*"

It was Master Elam. And by the surprised squeal that preceded his command, Jesse had seen him first, undoubtedly before she'd been fully dressed. Kit should have sensed him as soon as he came in. There was no excuse for this kind of distraction. Not today.

He found them in the hall of air. Jesse was tugging on her shirt behind Max, who'd taken a protective stance between her and his father. The usually stoic Elam was at full alert, his eyes focused like a hawk on his prey. And his prey was Jesse. "Step away from Jesse, Master Elam, and tell me what troubles you."

Elam's jaw tightened, but he took a step back. "The Beta has disappeared from the settlement. And it looks like he didn't leave empty handed."

Kit followed the direction of his gaze, his shock a physical blow when he realized the pedestal was empty. It was gone. "I know Dydarren well, Master. He is no thief."

"Then where is Legacy?"

From the corner of his eye he caught Jesse peering around Max's hip, biting her lip nervously. Hell. "Come here, Jesse."

She jumped at his tone, glaring at Max when he moved out of the way, no longer shielding her. God she was adorable, but Kit couldn't allow that to distract him. The stone was sacred to his people. If she knew anything… "Where did Jasyn go?"

She crossed her arms defensively, lifting her chin. "I don't know." Their silence made her shuffle. "I *don't*."

"Where's the stone that was on this pedestal?"

Her teeth dug into her lower lip, and she looked at the floor. "I think it's with my camera bag."

Kit ground his teeth together. Damn it. "Excuse us for a moment." He heard her breath catch when he slid his hands beneath her arms, picking her up off her feet and carrying her out of the room. He turned the corner and pressed her against the wall. "Start talking."

"I have no idea where Jasyn is, Kit, I swear. In the dream he just said that if all went well he'd see us soon."

The sharp dagger of jealousy pierced his heart. "You shared a dream with the pup last night? Tired of me so soon, angel?"

"No! No, it wasn't *that* kind of dream. He told me he had to go, that he had something he had to do."

What was she? He'd known of very few humans with supernatural abilities, the Readers came immediately to mind. But she wasn't a Reader. Yet, her ability to dreamwalk, to share his mind, could not be denied. "Did he steal it?"

"Why did Max's father call it Legacy?"

Kit's fingers tightened over her shoulders until she whimpered, making him realize what he was doing. "Legacy is the name of the stone, Jesse, and it is sacred to the Igigi. A gift to us from the Great Mother when she saved us from our creator. Did Dydarren steal it?"

Jesse struggled against him. "I don't think he stole it."

Kit started to relax, relief filling him until she spoke again, in a voice so hushed he had to lean in to hear her. "I think someone gave it to him."

He released her to pound against the wall above her head, rock dust whirling around them at the strength of his blow. He felt Max's firm grip on his shoulder, offering silent comfort and a much needed reminder of restraint.

He met Jesse's worried gaze. Betrayal tasted like bile in his mouth. What was Jasyn thinking? He knew they had sworn to help him escape with Jesse. How could he leave when he'd promised to protect her? Didn't he realize she wouldn't survive on her own? Did he not understand that there was no creature, Were or other, who could outrun or outlast the Igigi warriors when something this precious was at stake? "I cannot protect him now. The Beta's life is forfeit."

She covered her mouth, looking at Max for confirmation, and her eyes grew wide at his nod. Kit turned his back on her, unwilling to see her disappointment, her horror at the thought of Jasyn's demise.

He needed his control now more than ever. Getting her through an audience with the Old Ones without incident would be hard enough. His failure to protect the stone when it was right under his nose would not go unpunished. His mother would never allow it. She would be alert to any weakness, and she had a gift for finding them in others. If Jesse strayed from the role of random human, if his mother sensed he cared for her...then Great Mother help them both.

She had the strangest feeling that her underwear was showing. Everyone was staring at her as if she were the starring attraction at the flea circus. Jesse had never felt more uncomfortable in her life. Or shorter. She had to remind herself that most of them hadn't been this close to a human for hundreds of years. Some of the children, who were only slightly taller than her, had likely never encountered anyone outside the settlement at all.

Max had warned her to keep her eyes down and to stay close. It wasn't something he'd had to tell her twice. She still wasn't sure why Priestess Magriel had thought this was a good idea. Throwing her to the giants, like a hunk of raw meat to hungry wolves, seemed a recipe for disaster.

Yet, even on the way to her audience with the Old Ones, she couldn't stop thinking about Kit. He was angry and hurt at Jasyn's actions. She'd like to kick him in his wolfy head herself for putting her in this situation. He could have waited. Kit and Max had been planning to help him escape. But then, they wouldn't have allowed him to steal the stone.

And Kit's eyes when she'd mentioned dreaming of the Were. He'd acted like she'd been unfaithful. As if she had any control over her nighttime adventures. And yet, the Priestess, Regina and the others all thought that the dream sharing was her doing too.

It wasn't her. It couldn't be. She wasn't anything special, no matter what her mother had said.

"Don't be alarmed." That was all the warning she got from Max before she was lifted in the air. Her wrists, loosely tied by ropes once more before they'd exited the Halls of Record, flailed as she struggled to find her balance.

He set her on the flat surface of a stone column, so high that she could actually see over the Igigi's heads around her. They weren't staring at her anymore, instead, they were looking up.

Jesse turned and found herself eye level with one disturbingly hairy knee, ten times the size of her head. Good God. Her gaze was drawn up. And up. These were the creatures from all her childhood storybooks. These were the giants.

The Old Ones.

There were four in all, all dwarfing the mountain scenery behind them. Two men and two women, terrifying in their scope and scale. Jesse felt with a sudden certainty that she was going to die. Kit couldn't protect her from these beings. If he even wanted to after this morning.

"Before we get to any new business, I move we formalize our vote and inform the chosen of our decision."

Jesse's body vibrated from the power of the female voice. She covered her ears with her hands, until it stopped, surprise jarring her once more when Kit climbed the column beside her.

"I am ready."

An Old One smiled down at Kit. To Jesse he looked like Sir Laurence Olivier. Only...a giant version. She looked at the simple brown robe he was wearing, a robe that would probably blanket half the mountainside, and gulped. The elder man rubbed his white beard thoughtfully. "Always a clever one, Kittim. A warrior without equal. Our loss is great indeed. Know that the vote was not unanimous, and yet now we are in accord. You do a great service for your people by accepting."

Kit nodded, his expression grim when he turned his glance on the female who'd first spoken. "As my father before me, I hear and I obey."

"Yet you defied my orders for Kaine. So you obey, my son. But only when it suits you." Jesse looked at the woman in shock. My son?

She looked closer. The giantess was lovely. At first glance. Her knee-length robe a pristine white, her long dark braid threaded with silver. Maybe it was the tight mouth and narrowed eyes, but Jesse didn't see any family resemblance. Was this Amazon Kit's mother? She couldn't be. She was looking at him, not with love, but with open, unwavering hatred. Especially when he spoke again.

"My brother does not deserve the honor you bestowed, *Old One*. He has not trained to be a Sariel guard. He hasn't the ability to protect the Mediator. You were wrong to send him."

The murmurs rose up from the Igigi. No one spoke to the elders with such disrespect. But Kit wasn't done. "If I am to accept the mantle of *mahan calati*, then I also reap the benefits. I request the first of my boons. That my brother, Kaine, be barred from service as a Sariel guard. In that way we honor the blood oath my father took with the Trueblood clan, and serve them as loyally and faithfully as we always have, for as long as they need us."

The sneering man on this hillside beside Kit's mother shouted in anger, but the other Old Ones nodded in agreement. "You have your first boon, Kittim. Think hard before you request the other one."

Jesse felt eyes on her and turned. It was Kit's brother, Kaine. Now *he* looked exactly like his mother. He was speaking low in her ear, like a small devil on her shoulder, gazing at Jesse with wild eyes.

Kit's mother spoke. "Agreed. While he is thinking, we can deal with the other orders of business. The Beta will be caught soon enough, and his fate is sealed. We *do* need to address the human. We've been told it shared my son's mind, gleaning intelligence on the Sariels and Weres along the way."

It? "My name is Jesse. And I don't know why I—"

"You are *not* to speak unless spoken to." She was almost flung off the standing column with the power of the Old One's voice. Talk about being full of hot air. Jesse didn't care how big she was, that woman needed a lesson in manners.

"We should let her speak. Priestess Magriel has sent us all missives on her behalf, as you well know. I take her at her word that the human had no idea her dreams were real." Jesse smiled gratefully at the bearded elder to her left. He was obviously the kindest one of the bunch.

"The point is moot. A human cannot be allowed to leave with the knowledge she's been given, whether by accident or design. The decision to be made is merely death or imprisonment." Were all the female Igigi this irritating? Maybe it was because they were so outnumbered by the men. She glared at the blonde Old

One and glanced at Kit, waiting for him to say something on her behalf.

He didn't acknowledge the jab. And his mother noticed Jesse's reaction to his silence. "Kittim, do you wish to use your final boon to save the human? You have apparently been more than intimate with it if the facts are to be believed. You must care for the mortal."

"We have no control over our dreams, Old One. We can only be grateful when we wake. I will not use my boon on the human."

Jesse didn't care that everyone was looking at her. Some with pity. Others with outright glee. Let them look. Her heart felt like it was shattering apart. That he could stand here, in front of all his people, his family, and deny any feelings for her...she was on her own. Just as she'd always been.

Jesse stood taller, swallowing the painful lump in her throat. "You say Priestess Magriel has spoken for me. If you ask the guard who brought me to face you, he will admit that Zander and Regina Sariel, the people whom you have vowed to honor and protect, left him with an order to protect me from all harm."

The Old Ones turned to Max, who nodded as he stood guard at the base of her column. "She speaks the truth. They have affection for the human. They would be unhappy should she die."

"Thank you, Max. I could return to the Mediator. Under guard of course. The Vampires can thrall me out of any knowledge I've accidentally accumulated by getting my dream wires crossed with your warrior here. Trust me, I'd like to forget *all* of you exist as much as you want to forget me." Did Kit stiffen? Was he hurt by what she'd said? She'd like to think so. He deserved a little payback.

"She doesn't have to die, but how do we know she won't continue to have these dreams of hers after she leaves? There is, however, another solution. *I* will take her. Watch over her. I'll make sure she never endangers the security of our people. Since I've been banned from serving the Sariels, let me retain some measure of honor by taking her off all of your hands."

Jesse shuddered as Kit's brother drew everyone's attention. Kaine licked his lips, making it perfectly clear that his brand of babysitting was worse than any punishment her imagination could devise. Luckily, his mother seemed to be of the same mind.

"Don't be ludicrous, son. You have far more important things to do than play with this fragile creature. But you are right. She could become a danger again, even if the Sariels vouch for her. She will join Maximus, since he is the one who brought her to us. She will be a witness on Kittim's Great Walk."

"No!"

"Next to Kit, Maximus is our best warrior."

"What is the meaning of this?"

Voices swirled around her, all of them shocked at the Old One's decree. Kit had shouted an outright denial. He didn't want her with him? Well, that was fine. She just wanted out of this nightmare.

Max's father spoke up. "The *mahan calati* is no place for a human. And you do our people a great misdeed if you take *two* of the Igigi's best warriors away from us. I beg the Old Ones to rethink this. Surely you cannot all agree."

The dark skinned elder spoke for the first time, his worried expression matching Elam's. "It was agreed that, as the chosen is her eldest son, she would have the right to choose his witnesses. Although we had not expected this development."

Kit's mother waved her enormous hands, the wind blowing Jesse's glasses off her face. "Maximus cannot go against the Sariel's. He vowed to protect the human. *She* cannot be allowed to share the knowledge she has. Remember she has spent the night in the Halls of Record. Even though we protect them, are we willing to trust the Sariels with that knowledge? Do we trust them *that* much? No. It is the only way. I have made my choice."

"I request my second boon." Kit's loud voice silenced the whispering crowd. "I know I cannot change your decision. Instead I ask the three remaining elders to heed my words. I speak, not as the chosen but as one of you. Igigi. This council was chosen to keep us honest and just. To ensure that we did not slip into arrogance and lawlessness. That we would not be guided by our desire for vengeance and our greed. That path has led to the death of our people."

He sneered at his mother. "I submit to you that one among you does not follow that code. That you have been twice manipulated into choosing men whom she had already handpicked for her own selfish reasons. Her jealousy of her husband's power among you. And her fear that her eldest would thwart the plans she held for her beloved youngest son. Think hard when I am gone, before you allow her to manipulate you again. She has run out of family. The next chosen could be one of your heirs."

He leapt off the column and lifted the stunned Jesse in his arms while the crowd roared in surprise.

"I'm not sure that was wise, Kit."

Kit growled at Max, who was walking swiftly to keep up with him. "I am sick of wise. I didn't see it coming, Max. I never imagined she would pick you and—"

"I am honored to walk with you, my cousin. To the end."

Jesse felt her eyes mist despite her pique. She'd misjudged Max. He was a truly honorable warrior—unlike one other she'd decided never to speak to again. She untied the ropes that bound her and crossed her arms. Now that they were leaving she didn't see why she had to continue this charade.

Kit pushed his way past the crowd, not stopping until they reached the wooded entrance Jesse recalled from their arrival. Elam's face came into view. His expression as he looked at his son was tormented. "Remember when I told you of the warrior's choice?"

Max clenched his jaw, nodding jerkily. "I do, Master. Father, I will not let you down."

Elam took him by the shoulders and shook hard. "No, Maximus. You misunderstand me. I was wrong." He shared a speaking glance with Kit, shame in his eyes. “Very wrong. Be safe.”

The warriors nodded, pressing into the brush with silent speed. Neither men looked as though they would welcome questions about her luggage. Not that she cared. It was her camera bag she was steamed about. If Jasyn broke her camera...

She closed her eyes, holding herself away from Kit as much as she could while jostled about in his embrace. The images from her last dream filled her mind. The painting on the wall, all those bodies. Just a few hours before she’d been so determined to save him from that fate. She hadn’t changed her mind, but it was obvious now that he didn’t really want her with him. He thought of her as an anomaly, a fantasy made flesh. Attractive for a moment, but easily cast aside.

It hurt more because of all she’d seen. Weres and Truebloods sacrificing everything for their mates, laying down their lives to defend them. Kit couldn’t even do that. They weren’t made for love. Hadn’t he said that? They were warriors, artists, not monogamous life partners. She had to remember that. The best happy ending she could hope for would be to ensure that they didn’t follow the path in the painting. Getting home to her brother, his normal family, and that boring, vanilla accountant she was going to find and force herself to marry. Going back to the real world.

Where she belonged.

She had no inkling of how long they'd been traveling. They took a ferry, and Jesse looked on in amazement as people walked right past them, none of them seeing the two seven-foot, sword-wielding warriors and their bedraggled prize.

"It's called shadow stalking," Max told her. "It is a gift we can share with whomever we are in contact with. That's why they can't see or hear you."

"I could have used that for some of my more unusual assignments. Do you know how hard it is for a six-foot redhead to sneak up on a politician and his flavor of the month?" Jesse forced a wobbly smile for Max, falling into silence again as she watched the crowds mill about, unknowing.

At some point she must have fallen asleep in Kit's arms. When she woke up the moon was high. The air was warmer, dryer, but she couldn't tell where they were. The landscape was covered in shadows.

She was achy, hungry and she had to use the ladies' room. At this point she'd settle for a private bush. She looked over Kit's arm at Max. "Can we stop soon? I know you two aren't human, but I am and I need to...stretch my legs."

Kit looked at her, but she refused to meet his gaze, staring pointedly at his cousin. Max sent a questioning glance at Kit, before nodding to Jesse. "Not too long, but a few hours shouldn't hurt."

The moonlight helped lead the way to a small clearing, and Kit set her down, stepping away from her as though she were contagious. He made a gesture with his hands and disappeared into the tree line. Jesse went the opposite way with a little urgency.

When she returned, Max had already gathered firewood and was pulling a small flint from his belt. "You're like a boy scout." He smiled at her admiring tone, making quick work of the fire, until it blazed in front of her. She put her hands out to warm them. Heaven.

He'd rolled a fallen tree beside the blaze, gesturing for her to sit. "Thanks, Max. It's nice to know someone cares if I live or die. Speaking of insensitive jerks, where's Kit?"

Max's brow furrowed. "He's securing the area and finding food. Miss Jesse, I think you've gotten the wrong impression about Kit's actions today."

Jesse forced a laugh. "Wrong? I don't think so. He made his feelings crystal clear."

"No, he didn't. If he had, you would be dead by now. He was protecting you. From his brother, from the Old One, from all of them. Can't you see that?"

Max leaned closer to her, his expression adamant. "And still he couldn't hide it completely. We'd thought to get you away, to send you home. But we need a new plan. And we need it soon, before the true *mahan calati* begins."

Was that it? Had her own hurt feelings blinded her to the truth behind his actions? She'd wanted him to stand up for her, to show how he felt without shame. Had she been wrong?

"What is that? *Mahan calati*? I need to know what's happening. Please."

Max turned his gaze to the fire. "The Great Walk. This is only the third time it has happened since Great Mother took us under her care. The second time our leader, Kit's father, was chosen. Though I'm beginning to see that it was not a fair choosing. I'm beginning to see a lot of things."

He looked like his thoughts were a million miles away, but she needed information. "Max?"

"Our creator had a little trick up his sleeve before he agreed to let us go. When the stars align just right in his heaven, a warrior from the Igigi is chosen to honor him. The Great Walk is one of sacrifice, but it soothes the god's anger, and ensures peace for another two thousand years."

A flash of Kit's agonized face as he was felled by some unseen hand flashed behind her eyes. "Sacrifice? Why do I feel like you aren't talking about going without dessert here? Is Kit supposed to be the sacrifice?"

The look on Max's face was answer enough. "What kind of barbaric deal is that? How could this Great Mother allow it? I thought she'd decided you were worthy of saving?"

Max sighed. "She did, Jesse. She saved our race and your world from another global storm. The price is a single warrior every few millennia. It is not too high a toll to pay."

"It is for me." She couldn't do it. She couldn't watch Kit die, no matter how altruistic the motive. And she didn't understand how the people who said they cared about him, how the goddess who had done so much for all of her creations, could.

It was wrong.

Max started to reach for her, to soothe the distress she was so obviously feeling, but a rustling in the brush brought him to his feet.

Kit's expression appeared harsh in the light of the fire. What looked to be close to eight rabbits dangled from his fists. "Did I miss anything interesting?"

The prolonged silence caused his gaze to narrow on his cousin. "You told her."

Max lifted his chin. "She deserved to know."

"Yes, she did. And she's really glad someone is telling her something. Otherwise she'd have to whack someone over the head with a rock. Is that dinner? Please don't tell me we're eating Thumper's whole family." Kit, alerted by the change in her tone, turned his bottomless eyes her way. She sent him a small, hesitant smile, and watched his expression change to one of...relief?

His shoulders relaxed, and she knew that Max had been right. Kit cared that she'd been angry. He cared about her. Her smile widened and the side of his mouth tilted up in response.

Max chuckled. The sound was so rusty, so unusual that they turned to him in surprise. "What? I have a sense of humor." He blushed when they continued to stare. "Are we cooking the Thumper brood or not? I'm starving."

Chapter Eight

Jesse followed Kit into the woods. He'd told her there was a hot springs nearby, a place where she could wash, but she knew he just wanted to get her alone. He'd been staring at her all through dinner, the heated look in his eyes making it clear that he wanted to pick up where they'd left off last night, before the audience with the Old Ones, before the misunderstandings.

But she wasn't sure she could go back. Not now that she knew where they were going. Where he was going. How much more could she invest her heart with a man who wouldn't be around tomorrow, or the next day? A man who would leave her, just as surely as her father abandoned his family.

"You're unusually quiet, *sarasvatti.* I find I miss your constant observations."

Jesse chuckled. "Are you saying I talk too much?"

They reached the hot springs, and he stopped her before she could run into a large boulder hiding the pool. He met her gaze. "No. In fact, I wanted to say...you were very brave today. Not many humans could accept this world, let alone hold their own within it."

She blushed. "Well, it wasn't all new to me. I've spent half a lifetime dreaming of you, and the other half wishing the dreams were real. Although I admit I wasn't expecting to butt heads with a council of Goliaths. That part was new."

"I'm sorry I put you through that." He released her and took a step back, into the darkness. "I should have protected you. Should have found a way to get you out with Dydarren. My greed to have more time with you has put you in greater danger."

She shook her head. "I'm glad I stayed, but what do you mean? We're out here in the middle of nowhere. No one would know if I—if both of us—chucked this Great Walk thing and went to Tahiti. Sounds like a plan to me."

"Would that it were true, my angel. But from the moment I accepted the path chosen by the Old Ones, we have not been alone. I can sense them, stirring along the perimeter of our camp."

"Sense who?"

"The creator's beasts. Two of his earlier creations that guard his abode of thunder and carry out his wishes. Don't worry, *sarasvatti*. As long as you are with us they will not hurt you. But they will not let you go until we reach our final destination. It is only then that you and Max will have a chance to leave."

The creator's beasts? Her mind raced to fill in the horrifying blanks. She'd seen some of his earlier creations in the wall relief back at the settlement. Each one was more terrifying than the next. One of those was out there watching them? She shuddered.

This was going to make her plan to save the day a little more difficult. "You and Max can't fight them?"

Kits harsh laugh made her jump. He'd moved closer in the darkness. "Oh, we could fight them. But the outcome isn't as assured as you're hoping. Trust me, angel. Just stay close to Max when the time comes. He will keep you safe. Now please, no more talk of things we cannot change. I think the time has come to teach you about underestimating me."

Jesse yelped as her clothes disappeared. "A little warning would be nice."

"I'm not feeling nice, *sarasvatti*." Kit came closer, a predatory expression on his face. "You didn't trust me. Didn't trust I was doing what I needed to do to keep you safe."

She stumbled backward, her back hitting the smooth, damp boulder behind her. "I trust you."

Kit shook his head. "You trust me with your body. Your pleasure. That is all." He slid her glasses slowly off her face. "I want everything."

He took off his shirt, unbuckling his sword and sliding out of his pants. The simple act of undressing seemed slower and more torturous because of his unused ability. He was teasing her. Showing her one patch of muscled, lickable skin at a time. The moonlight caressed his body, dancing softly over his mammoth erection. Her heart skipped.

She was in serious trouble.

Kit sat beside the hot springs, his calves disappearing inside the steaming water. He crooked his finger. "Come here."

"Why?"

A growl emerged from the darkness. "*Sarasvatti.* Come. Here."

Jesse stepped closer, hesitant, until her breasts were touching his broad shoulders. Her stomach fluttered, the way it always did when she was near him. His size overwhelmed her.

"You've been a bad girl, angel. Bend over my lap and take your punishment."

"Oh God." She wondered, not for the first time, if there wasn't something wrong with her. Especially when she obeyed his command without hesitation, her body already shaking with desire at the knowledge of what he was about to do.

Her hands slid in the damp earth surrounding the natural spring as she curved her body over his hot thighs. A layer of steam coated her body, her nipples hardening from the sensation.

"I should deny you, since that would be a true punishment. But I have no wish to deny myself. I want to see your cheeks glowing a rosy red, feel you squirming in delight against me, hear you beg for more. Beg, Jesse. Beg for your spanking."

She shook her head wildly, her whole body quivering as she sought to wait him out. He cupped the curve of her hip, tempting her. She wanted to beg, so badly. Wanted to feel her clit throb with every sharp sting. But some contrary part of her mind demanded she resist.

"I wish I could hear your thoughts, little one. The only time I know what you want from me is when we are like this, and even here you seek to refuse me." His other hand slid beneath her to cup her aching breast, his fingers clamping around the nipple, so tightly she jerked in his arms with a jagged cry. "Beg, *sarasvatti.* Beg for my hand, my cock. Beg for whatever I want to do to you, however I want it. Or I end this now."

"Please. Please, Kit. Spank me. Fuck me. I need it. Need you."

"Yes." He soothed her breast with gentle fingers, the hand on her hip lifting before coming down with a satisfying smack on her left cheek. Then her right. Again and again his cupped hand fell against her flesh, until Jesse was mindless with arousal, her body on fire for more.

Her cream coated her sex, her thighs. She spread her legs, arching her hips to beg for his hand there, where she needed him most. The spanking stopped, and she felt his rough fingers caressing her clit, sliding through the lips of her pussy. "I love how hot you are. So much fire in such a little package."

Jesse moaned when two of his fingers entered her pussy, pumping in and out slowly. Too slowly. She was going insane. "Please."

"I know what you need, angel." He withdrew his fingers from her sex, the soaked digits tracing the sensitive skin, moving until they slipped between the cheeks of her ass. He pressed against the tight ring of muscles while Jesse let out a shocked cry. "Will you give me what I need?"

"Won't. Fit." It was hard to concentrate, the sensation of his wet fingers pushing persistently against her, there, threw her mind into chaos. She couldn't possibly take him there. Could she?

"It will. You know it will. Breathe, Jesse. Relax." His voice lowered. "Trust me."

Jesse took a deep breath, focusing on relaxing her muscles, and felt the hand against her shake. "That's it, *sarasvatti*. You're so beautiful, my angel. So beautiful and open to my touch."

The stinging spank across the lips of her sex took her by surprise and sent her careening into the atmosphere. Every nerve in her body was on fire, hypersensitive to each sensation. When Kit's finger pushed through the resistance and filled her ass, it was too much.

Her climax racked her body, jolting her over and over again as he fingered her ass with long, slow strokes. She could hear him muttering softly under his breath, and she struggled to understand the words.

"Great Mother. Fuck, Jesse your ass is so tight, so hot and tight, baby...I need to..." Kit wrapped his arms around her and slid them both into the heated spring, her back pressed against his chest.

She gripped the forearm braced above her breasts, opening her mouth on his skin as he sunk his fangs into her neck. She came again, screaming against his flesh and biting him in return.

The growl against her neck was feral. Kit tightened his grip on her hip, pulling her back until his thick cock was pressed between the cheeks of her ass. Oh God. She wanted it. It was dirty and kinky, but she wanted him to fill her there more than anything. She didn't know if it was the drugging effect of his fangs, and she didn't care. "Yes, Kit. Yes."

He couldn't hold back. His bite was the closest he ever came to sharing Jesse's mind and emotions, and each time the link seemed to grow more intense. With her blood trickling like honey down his throat, and her body pressed against his, they were one. Kit could feel the aftereffects of her climax, the waves of her arousal already rising inside her once more. She was driving him to distraction. And as much as he wanted it, the images flowing through his mind, images of him powering into her ass, forcing her to take his cock, were not his own.

Kit didn't question how he knew, or the impossibility of their link. He gloried in it. That he could share this with her, if nothing else. He prodded her tight asshole with the head of his cock, injecting her with as much of the relaxant his fangs could excrete. He needed her, needed to take her hard and deep, but the last thing he wanted was for her to feel true pain.

She came against him, and he felt the head of his cock pulse, his shaft growing with his arousal. He couldn't wait another minute. As her body shuddered against his in the churning water, he pushed through the snug heat of her ass, feeling it give and stretch as inch by hard, aching inch he slowly filled her.

Hearing his name on Jesse's lips, the sound a weak whimper in her throat, forced him to pull his fangs from her flesh and lick the wound. Had he taken too much? "*Sarasvatti*, my love, are you all right?"

Please Goddess let her be all right. He would rather die than end this feeling. Her luscious ass clung so sweetly to his erection, he'd never felt anything like it. Anything like her.

A picture flashed in his mind. An image of his fingers fucking her pussy while his hips pumped against her ass. Hers? But how? They were no longer connected. How was it he could still sense her desires?

Kit slid a hand down the front of her body, his fingers ran through her waterlogged curls and slipped into her sex, the fiery sheath gripped his fingers like a fist. "Fuck, angel. Is this what you wanted?"

"Yes. I can feel you everywhere."

He licked her neck, his hips dragging backward while his fingers pressed deep. Jesse shouted, her hips jerking against him. "Slow down, baby. I've got you." He slung his hips forward, going deeper. "I've wanted this for so long, angel. Every time you showed up in my dreams with that scrap of sex and lace barely covering your curves, I wanted to bend you over and spread you wide. Wanted to make you mine in every way there is."

"Ohgodohgodohgod."

Kit smiled against her skin, loving how hot he could make her. Loving that she was just as aroused as he. He quickened his pace, arching his neck with a groan when her internal muscles tightened around him.

He wasn't going to last. He added a third finger to the two already inside her pussy, determined to hear her cries of ecstasy once more before he came. He scraped her shoulder with his fangs. "Now I'm the one begging, angel. *Sarasvatti.* Please, Jesse. Don't make me wait anymore."

It was Kit who shouted as Jesse's body quaked in climax. The explosion ripped through his system, blending with his own, intensifying every sensation. Her stunned scream told him she was experiencing the same merging. That she felt every powerful jerk of his cock as he came inside her, every flash of fire through his veins.

He pulled out carefully, eyes closing to absorb every last spasm. He turned the sobbing Jesse in his arms and rocked her gently in the warm water. Kit allowed himself a moment of heartache when he felt Jesse's emotions fade from his mind. But only a moment. The Great Mother had gifted him again, allowing him a chance to experience a connection similar to that of his charges and their mates. Unity. With the human who held his heart just as surely as any bloodbound mate.

Jesse.

Like all the gifts from his Goddess, Jesse came with a catch. She'd walked out of his dreams, proving to be more desirable in the flesh than any fantasy. She was courageous, smart, and utterly adorable with those big glasses that she thought distracted people from her stunning emerald eyes. And it was killing him that he couldn't keep her. Couldn't take her tonight and run. Somewhere where the Igigi would never find them. But it was impossible.

He took a deep breath and smelled them. The gatekeepers who were watching to ensure the *mahan calati* was completed. Master Elam had told him and Max about them after he'd returned from escorting Kit's father on his Great Walk. He'd never seen his Master intimidated by anything. A warrior never showed fear, but Elam had come close when he described his first sighting of the beasts.

"Kit?"

"Yes, angel?" He focused on the bundle in his arms, her body flushed pink and glowing in the moonlight. Beautiful. Except for the furrow wrinkling her brow.

"I can't stop thinking of a dream I remember. In it you stopped time, or at least, slowed it down. Was that real?"

He knew where she was going. "It doesn't matter, Jesse. I can't stop it forever, no matter how much I wish it would."

She pulled away, splashing toward the edge of the small pool without a word. He clothed her in his shirt as soon as she stood, shivering and naked on solid ground.

It clung to her damp body, the sleeves dangling past her hands to her knees. She looked like an innocent child. Until he studied her expression. He didn't need to read her mind to know she was disappointed by his answer. Disappointed in him.

He leapt from the hot springs, heedless of the water pouring down his large frame. "*Sarasvatti.* You have to understand. An Igigi warrior, a Sariel guard is nothing if he does not fulfill his duty. I have *never* shirked mine, not in well over three thousand years." Her eyes grew wide. "I have fought in more wars than I can count, and done things in the name of duty that I didn't agree with, but I have never hesitated. Never even thought about it. And I never had a single regret."

Kit cupped her face in his hands and sighed. "Until you, Jesse. I love you, angel. But no matter how I feel about you, there is too much at stake for me to pick this moment to be selfish. It goes against all my training. And without that, I am no better than Kaine. And I'd be no good for you."

Jesse sighed, her eyes closing for a moment, hiding her thoughts from him. "We should get back." She turned, leaving his hands hovering over empty air. Before she disappeared on the path, she stopped with her back to him. "Humans are just not as evolved as the Igigi, I suppose. At least, I'm not. I'd rather have love than honor. Rather die than bow before a god who didn't deserve my worship. And I would never leave someone I claimed to love alone by choice. Not like my father did. No. I'd fight with every breath in my body, god of thunder or no, before I let that happen."

Kit felt every word like a knife in his heart. Did she think that this was easy for him? Leaving the one thing in this endless life that he'd ever wanted for himself? His honor, his training, they were the only things that kept him from damning the world to a watery grave. Why couldn't she see that he was doing this for her? For her species, just as much as his own.

He forced himself to don the mask of the Sariel guard, clothing himself and grabbing his sword and her glasses before he stepped in front of her on the path. "I'm not human, Jesse. And because I'm not, you will survive. I hope when this is over, you remember that."

He heard her shuffling slowly behind him, and she didn't say another word until they reached his cousin tending the fire. She spoke softly to Max and he nodded, looking at Kit with an apologetic glance that was easy to interpret. Jesse was hurting. Because of him.

Kit clothed her with a thought, replacing his damp shirt for her buttoned up blouse and jeans. He strode to the other guard, slipping Jesse's glasses into his hand. "She'll need these. You two go on ahead, I'll catch up once the fire is out."

"Kit..."

"Go, Max. Tomorrow will come soon enough, and we have a way to go to reach our destination."

He watched Max swing Jesse up in his arms, his jaw tight as he fought not to shout a denial. She was his. She belonged to him.

After tomorrow you'll be gone. Who will she belong to then?

Kit put out the fire with slow, methodical movements. He felt the rage building inside him with every passing moment. At his mother. At fate for bringing Jesse to him only to tear her away. And most of all, at the god who still demanded blood to appease his fragile ego.

The beasts were close. Hovering in the darkness. They were so close he could hear the flap of wings, the click of claws on the ground. Kit allowed himself to shift, growing larger as they watched. "If you want a fight, you have one. I'm not in the mood to be threatened."

They stilled.

"No. I didn't think so. You have to keep me alive, don't you? He wouldn't appreciate you getting ahead of yourselves and killing the sacrifice meant for him."

Kit wasn't sure how long he stood there, his fangs bared in warning, his head above the tree line. He watched Max carry Jesse through the thick woods, feeling his heart cracking a little more with every mile that grew between them.

He rubbed the scar on his chest. The mark that still appeared on all the Igigi at birth. The one burned off during adolescence to ensure no trace would be left behind—the god's mark. The stamp he left in their genetic code, a lightning bolt to show his mastery over the storm.

How long would they have to pay for the accident of their birth? He turned to the monsters scuffling impatiently behind him.

"I have a message for your god."

The sun was rising in the Syrian Desert. Jesse had been here before, to photograph the Bedouins who called this harsh Eden home. She and Max had traveled far, and much faster than they had when going to the Igigi lands. It seemed Max had slowed down for Jasyn's sake. It was overwhelming to think of the abilities Kit's people had.

Kit. He'd remained behind them the rest of the journey, though Max had assured her he was close. He didn't need to. Something had happened the last time Kit had bitten her. It didn't make any sense, but then, neither had the dreams. She could feel him. His emotions, his thoughts. It was as if all she had to do was think of him, and he was there, in her mind.

Why? He'd told her the Igigi didn't mate the way Weres and Truebloods did, that they weren't made that way. And she knew it was true. If it wasn't, he would have known that it was fear of losing him that had driven her last night. That what she wanted more than anything was to have him beside her, sharing what little time they had left. Apparently their new connection was one-sided.

She understood now exactly what was at stake, why he couldn't refuse. And without a doubt, she knew that he would turn his back on the world to be with her, despite his beliefs, if she asked him again. She'd fought with herself all night not to do just that. But how could she? She thought about her brother Adrian and his family, about all the people she'd photographed through the years, in compromising positions and out, and she knew she couldn't be that selfish.

There had to be another way.

Jesse knew the instant Kit appeared beside them. He didn't glance her way, his expression so stoic that if she didn't know how he truly felt about her, she'd think he didn't know she existed.

"Max, keep her here. No matter what you see."

"Of course, my cousin. May our Great Mother protect you."

"Wait! What—" Kit walked down the dune without another word, his jaw set, hand on the hilt of his sword.

"He goes to face his first challenge. To prove he is worthy to be the Igigi sacrifice."

Jesse's stomach dropped. "You have to be fucking kidding me. Who the fuck *is* this egomaniacal jackass? How dare he test Kit's worth? Or any of your people's? Hell, Kaine is worth more than that jerk."

Max's laugh sounded surprised. "Bite your tongue. The Beta mentioned you had a mouth on you."

"Only when I'm angry. Is this test dangerous?" She wrapped her arms around her waist, as if to protect herself from his answer. She didn't blink, refusing to take her gaze from Kit's shrinking figure. If she couldn't protect him, the least she could do was bear witness.

“Not for the trained warrior. My father told me that there are two challenges before the final ritual. This first is merely to test the senses and physical prowess. The second tests the heart and mind. I do not think the god made these tests to harm our people. After all, if Kit died here then he wouldn’t have the same...satisfaction.”

She heard the distaste in his voice. It was a feeling she shared. The monster from the stele on the wall, the one so petty and filled with hatred that he demanded something like this from his children, was no god. Not by her definition. And if she knew where to find him, she’d tell him so.

Kit had come to a swift stop, his head tilted as if scenting something on the wind. He turned in a slow circle, sliding out his sword and gripping it in both hands.

Jesse gasped, reaching for Max’s arm. “He’s facing the wrong way. Why is he facing the wrong way?”

Max inhaled sharply, turning her to face him. “Jesse, what do you mean? I sense the same enemy Kit does, but not in any discernible direction.”

“You don’t see them?”

“Them?”

Chapter Nine

Kit was on edge, but not because of the upcoming challenge. He'd spent the night in hell, watching the woman he loved in another's arms. He trusted his cousin, but there was no doubt he desired Jesse. And like a fool, he'd accepted Max's oath to take care of her after Kit was gone.

How long would Max wait before comforting Jesse turned into something more? Was he so selfish that he begrudged her happiness with another, even when he wouldn't be around to take care of her? He wished he could say no.

A profound stench stopped him in his tracks. His skin crawled in the same way it had when the god's creatures began following them. But the smell told him this was something else. Something decidedly older. And if he wasn't mistaken, it wasn't alone.

He drew his sword and reached out with his senses. He couldn't see anything, and his sense of smell was no indicator of direction. The odor surrounded him, coming from everywhere at once. Where were they? What were they?

"Kit! Kit, can you hear me? Please, for the love of your goddess, tell me you can hear me."

Kit spun toward the rise of the dune. Jesse hadn't moved, Max had kept his word. So why did he hear her as clearly as if she were standing right beside him.

"Jesse?"

"Kit? Oh, thank goodness. I see—"

"How are you doing this? How can we be talking telepathically?"

"I don't know, but can't it wait? I can see them, Kit. I can see the things surrounding you. Kit, they're all around you!"

He lifted his sword high, whirling, but he saw nothing. *"Describe it to me. What do they look like? How many?"*

"There are four of them. They are nearly half as big as your Old Ones, and they look like men, sort of, except for their tails. Kit, they have scorpion tails. Oh, shit."

"Be calm, sarasvatti. *They are Agrabuamelu, children of the dragon. I heard tales of them at my father's knee. Thank you, Jesse. Now quiet your thoughts, my love."*

Ancient indeed. Earlier creations that had been, for the most part, forgotten. His people had thought them lost in the flood. They were not supposed to have powers of invisibility. That must be a recent addition.

Kit closed his eyes, knowing them worthless, and listened. His father had told him the stories. That their terror was awesome, their glance like poison, and their sting deadly. But their tails were cumbersome things, noisy. And once they'd been cut off, the beasts were easy enough to kill, since they had no mental dexterity, no free will.

If the stories were true.

He heard a whirring to his left, loud as a helicopter to his alert senses, and rolled to the ground. His blade followed the noise, the slice of connection and screech of pain telling him he'd found his mark. One down.

"Ew. The tail is still twitching and that, um, Agra-whatsit is crawling away, Kit. The other three are spreading out around you."

"You may want to avert your eyes, angel."

"Then how would I help you?"

The real question was, why would she want to? She had made her feelings clear last night. She didn't approve of what he was doing. And how in the name of the Mother could she be talking to him? The small connection they'd shared during sex had faded along with his orgasm.

The sand shifted beside him and he jumped high, his boot connecting to flesh with a satisfying crunch. A powerful hand gripped his neck, keeping his feet of the ground and pulling him forward. The aroma grew stronger, making his eyes water.

This creature was strong, and while Kit struggled to peel its fingers off his throat, a fist slammed into the small of his back. Damn. He roared, his fangs extending with the pain.

"Kit! The third one's tail is arching, it looks like...like... Move left. Now!"

He wrenched himself to the left, loosening the scorpion hybrid's hold just in time. He heard the sickening sound of a stinger piercing flesh, luckily not his own, and smiled grimly. Once more his sword slid through the thick armored tail, currently stuck to the chest of his brethren. A thudding sound, followed by a large dip in the revealing sand and he knew he'd hit his target. *"Thanks,* sarasvatti.*"*

"I'm gonna be sick. One more, Kit. But he's the biggest one yet. And he looks pissed."

Not pissed enough. Kit stilled, breathing deep as he honed in to the sounds around him. He could hear the scratching of hands in sand, crawling away, the whimpers of a poisoned soul dying in the morning heat. And he could hear the harsh breath of anger, the stalking glide of the final Agrabuamelu, determined in his vengeance.

"Why do you hide from me, my brother? Are you a coward that you cannot face another of our god's creations? Do you believe yourself inferior? I'm not sure why I'm talking to you. Can you even understand my words, or weren't you given that ability?"

The air shimmered to Kit's right, and he turned in time to watch the scorpion man appear in the flesh. He did not look completely formed. His forehead was lumped with horns, his nose merely a vertical slit below his lidless eyes. Kit looked away from his glance, focusing instead on his weapon. Long and large, covered in scales that glowed red in the light of dawn, his tail was a thing of beauty. A perfect killing machine.

"Ah. So you understand after all. Why would you hide from this battle? The sight of your face alone is so revolting you could have stunned me in my tracks."

The extended jaw opened and a blood curdling sound was released, knocking Kit back with its power. The sound rang in his ears, making him weave, disoriented. The thick tail rippled, pushing the thing closer, within striking distance.

"Kit! Concentrate. He's... Oh my God."

He shouted out in pain as the stinger skewered his shoulder. He shifted, his body stretching and elongating. His muscles grew too, pressing out the sharp point until it fell, blood soaked on the ground. But he could already feel the poison flowing through his veins. There wasn't much time.

He towered above the Agrabuamelu, whose tail was flopping wildly, reacting to the loss of its stinger. Kit reached down with his large fist, pounding the enemy into the sand. He fumbled with the tiny stinger, now the size of a hangnail, and pressed it into the squealing creature's forehead with his thumb.

Kit turned to gaze at Jesse one last time as a wave of nausea consumed him, bringing him hard to his knees. Something was wrong. This was not how the challenge was supposed to end. Perhaps this was his creator's answer to his message.

Jesse. He thought he'd have more time. One more day. He wanted to tell her he was sorry. Wanted to hold her in his arms and tell her how much he loved her.

"I know, you big behemoth. Now stay still until we can get to you and get that poison out."

"Can't. Too late. Jesse, I—"

"Don't say it, Kit. Just rest. It's going to be okay. I can't let you go. Not yet."

He awoke with a bitter taste in his mouth. His head was lead heavy on the ground. Kit groaned, and immediately felt a cool cloth cover his aching brow. "Kit? Kit, can you hear me?"

"Jesse?"

"I'm here. Max carried us for hours. Wouldn't take no for an answer."

Kit grimaced. This was no time for the green monster. And no one deserved it less than Max. He was alive. And Jesse, his angel, was leaning over him with love in her eyes. "How long?"

Max answered. "The sun is still hours from setting." His voice sounded strange, as strange as his answer. Kit struggled to a sitting position and rubbed his eyes.

"How?" How had the Agrabuamelu not killed him? He knew of no antidote, and the venom itself was meant to work nearly instantaneously. How had he survived?

"It was Jesse."

She huffed, glaring at Max over her shoulder. "It was not, damn it." She turned to Kit. "He's back to thinking I'm a crazy witch. I think you have some friends in high places. When we got to you your lips were blue and your face was clammy. I saw a flash and *it* appeared on the ground beside you. A vial full of liquid. I gave it to you and you got your color back immediately, though you didn't wake up. Max brought us here."

He felt his brow furrow in disbelief. A vial appeared? The god he knew of would never do that. The Mother was forbidden from interfering in this ritual sacrifice. He didn't know what to think except... "You spoke telepathically. You saw the scorpion men when I could not."

She stood and planted her hands on her hips. "If I hadn't, you'd be dead. Look, I'm just as confused as you, but I'm not sorry. If I hadn't been able to reach your mind..." She shuddered. "I didn't make an antidote appear from nowhere for heaven's sake. I'm human. Remember?"

Max snorted. "You smell human. You act human. But the dreams, and now this? Something is going on. And it all centers around you."

Kit held up his hand. "Max is just worried, angel. For both of us. And in case you hadn't figured it out yet, he hates surprises. And that's exactly what this challenge was."

"That was no challenge. It was an ambush. My father told me yours fought a single ancient beast. And it was not hidden from view."

Kit stood, nodding as Jesse slid her small body under his arm for support. "I agree. I think I've made you-know-who a little angry. Angry enough that he's trying to ensure

I don't pass the challenges. And if I don't, you know what happens."

Max dipped his head in agreement but Jesse pulled back to look him in the eye. "He's cheating? Who is this guy, anyway? For an immortal he sounds a lot like a two-year-old."

Kit laughed despite his discomfort. Great Mother, how he loved this woman. He didn't care who or what she was. She was his. And that was all that mattered. He looked around, his heart growing heavy at the sight of the ruins. His father had told him of this place, and of its destruction.

"Baalbeck. The next challenge is held on his own sacred ground. It would be a stretch, even for him, to 'cheat' here."

"Baalbek. As in Lebanon? We're already in Lebanon? And wait...Baal? The god who created you is Baal? Holy shit."

Max tilted his head. "Do you know of him?"

Jesse shrugged. "My brother was more into mythology in school than I was. But that sounds familiar. Doesn't Baal just mean 'lord'?"

"Yes. His real name is—"

"Kit." Max took a step forward. An instinct, Kit knew. It was ingrained in all of them. Only Baal's high priests could call him by his true name.

Kit shrugged. "He was known as Baal, god of thunder and the storm. Jupiter, Zeus, he took whatever name suited him at the time. Only a privileged few knew his true moniker."

Jesse bit her lip. "So this place..."

"The Igigi built a temple city in honor of him here. It reached the heavens, more intricate than the Halls of Record, more massive in scope than any before or since. It was here he directed his wrath at the onset of the flood. It leveled everything but the foundation. The Romans and others reclaimed and rebuilt on its foundation, still honoring him, but those civilizations fell as well."

"It must really irk him that no one comes to worship him anymore."

Kit shared a look with Max. Jesse had a way of putting things. After thousands of years of subtlety, blunt was a refreshing change. It just took a little getting used to. But Kit had thought the exact same thing. For a god like Baal, being forgotten was far worse than being despised.

"So what happens now?"

He caressed her cheek, pushing up the glasses that had slipped down her nose. "At sunset we enter what remains of the temple. And then I face the second challenge."

She leaned into his touch, a watery smile on her plump lips. "*We'll* face the second challenge."

"Of course. How can I lose with my guardian angel at my side?"

Maybe it was all the waiting. Or the fact that tourists were milling around taking pictures like something horrific wasn't about to happen. Whatever the reason, Max was ticking her off.

"Quit looking at me like that, Maximus."

Max jerked, startled. "What?"

She stomped her feet, careful to keep one hand on the sitting Kit's shoulder, so that she didn't scare the unknowing humans by appearing from thin air. "You know what. Like you did when we first met, like I was some sort of pervert. Or three-headed alien. I don't know why I could see them, okay? I don't know why I dreamed of Kit, knew what Jasyn was going to do or talked to my mother, who's been dead for nearly a decade."

Jesse took a shaky breath, leaning against Kit as the strangeness of it all hit her. "Nothing like this has ever happened to me before. But if you keep staring at me like I might shrink you to the size of a toadstool, well, I might just give it a shot."

"Whoa, angel. Max is a little tense, but truthfully, he's staring because he's remembering you naked, and wishing he'd gotten to watch how hard you came when I filled your ass with my cock last night."

Now it was Jesse's turn to be shocked. Instinctively she looked around, blushing, to see if anyone had heard. Kit chuckled. "No one can see or hear us, *sarasvatti.* Not as long as one of us is touching you. Does that excite you? The idea of being bad in public? You can do anything you want, angel, and no one will know."

He was the devil. That was the only explanation for her reaction to his sinful words. She caught a glimpse of Max from the corner of her eye. His cheeks were flushed, but he didn't walk away. Both men breathed her in and she shivered, recalling how exciting it was to have sex with Kit while Max looked on.

"I'm thinking after the beating I've taken today, I might not be able to give you what you need. Not alone."

Jesse used her newfound ability. *"Kit, you better not be talking about what I think you're talking about."*

"You know I am. You can read my mind, after all."

"I thought you didn't want to share me. I thought I was yours."

Kit gave a mental growl. *"You are mine. That will never change. He can't have you. Not the way I do. But don't lie and pretend you haven't imagined four hands caressing you, a mouth on each breast. That you haven't thought about Max doing more than watching. Goddess knows he has. I've smelled it on him from the moment he brought you to me. I've been jealous nearly as long."*

Jesse frowned. *"But you aren't anymore?"*

"You love me. You've been angry with me, you've been afraid for me...but you love me. I felt it while I was inside you. And because of your special gifts, denying how I feel would be foolish." He tugged her hips closer, nipping her breast through her thin shirt. *"I want to be the one to give you this. To make all your fantasies come true. Trust me once more,* sarasvatti. *With your body and your heart."*

He sensed her soften and turned toward Max. “Will you help me pleasure my mate?” His cousin’s eyes widened, whether at the term “mate” or the offer, Jesse wasn’t sure which, but after a moment, he dipped his chin in a short nod.

“Good. Let’s get rid of all this.” Kit removed all their clothes with a grin, keeping a firm grip on Jesse when it felt as though she might bolt. “Stay close, angel. One of us must touch you at all times, else you’ll give the natives quite a show.”

The two men were sitting on broken columns in the grass under the shadow of Jupiter’s Temple. Baal’s, she corrected herself. They were like a painting. Art her camera could never catch, regardless of her talent.

Two ageless Igigi warriors, giants, their bodies made for war. Both of them looking at her as though she was the most beautiful thing they’d seen in a thousand years. It was heady.

And Kit. She could see inside his mind, the demons he was trying to overcome. His struggle between what was right and what he wanted. He was in pain. He needed her, needed this, to celebrate life, when hours before he’d been so close to death.

Jesse slid her hand down his chest, kneeling on the ground between his thighs. His eyes narrowed. Good. Everything didn’t have to follow his plans. Besides, as much as he wanted her pleasure, she wanted his. “Let me.”

She wrapped both hands around the base of his hardening cock. Her fingers barely touched and she shuddered, thinking of how good it felt to have him deep inside her, still in awe that she could take him at all.

"Angel, you don't have to do this." Kit's voice was rough with arousal. His cock pulsed in her hand, filling with blood and desire at the mere thought of her mouth on him. She visualized what she wanted to do to him, trying to send the image into his mind. He groaned aloud, and she knew she'd done it.

She loved this. Loved being connected with him this way. And it kept getting easier. After her terror during his last challenge, when she'd forced a shared link between them to help, her senses had become more attuned to his, his emotions easier and easier to read. She had no idea why it was happening, but she wasn't about to question this kind of gift. Not if it meant she could have that much more of him. As long as she had him.

His callused fingers lifted her chin, his gaze filled with the same yearning. She pulled back, just enough to kiss the fingers, bending forward to press her lips gently on the head of his cock. It was warm, like heated velvet against her mouth. Her tongue slipped out to taste, and her eyes closed. It was salty, dark, and something so vitally him that she had to have more.

Her mouth opened wide around him, her tongue lapping at his shaft, struggling to taste every, delicious inch.

"Sweet Goddess, *sarasvatti.* Your mouth is heaven. Just as hot and sweet as your pussy, angel. Spread your legs and let Max have a taste."

Jesse stiffened, her mouth full, eyes going wide as she felt a new pair of hands caressing her back, the cheeks of her ass. *"Kit?"*

"Relax, my love. He won't do any more than taste and touch. Let me give you this. Let us."

She spread her legs, whimpering against his shaft when she felt Max's hand dip between her thighs to cup her sex.

"She's soaking wet." Max sounded as though he was choking. His fingers were shaking slightly, and Jesse instinctively arched, pressing herself harder against his hand.

"Wait until you taste her. Nothing can compare to her sweet honey." Jesse sucked hard, trying to distract him enough to stop him from talking. It was driving her crazy. Her body was as taut as a bowstring, quivering as she waited for what would happen next.

Max shifted, and then she was crying out as she felt his hot breath against her clit. He was on his back, his head between her knees, hands on her hips. He squeezed gently. He was asking, allowing her to set the pace.

"Oh, yes, Jesse. Your mouth...that's right, baby, suck my cock while Max fucks your sweet pussy with his tongue."

Oh God. She tried to take more of him, sliding her fists up and down his thick width, but he was big. She let her hips lower toward Max's mouth, too turned on to be embarrassed.

At the first slow, lick of his tongue, she lifted her gaze to Kit's. It was different. Max was gentle, reverent, not as confident at what she needed as Kit had always been. But it felt...exciting and forbidden. Wonderful. And Kit knew.

"She likes it, Max. I think she wants more. Wants her pussy filled with your tongue. Don't you, angel? Want every hole you have stuffed with us while the world goes on around us, unknowing."

She'd forgotten. Forgotten that there were tour groups and archaeology students, families wandering the ruins while she was reveling in her newfound sexual debauchery. She heard laughter close by, a professor was talking about Roman architecture, and Max lost all hesitation, shoving his tongue deep inside her pussy with a purr of pleasure.

Jesse could feel Kit's cock probe the back of her throat. And there was much of him she had yet to taste. She wished she could take more. She lifted one hand from his erection, raising it to his lips. "Bite me, Kit. I want more of you."

"Fuck, angel. Yes." He wrapped his fingers around her arm, pulling her wrist to his mouth and biting down. Jesse's body tingled, her blood on fire. She breathed out, her throat opening so she could take more, swallowing the head of his cock down her throat.

Kit's other hand gripped her hair convulsively, his hips lifting, pushing himself even further into her mouth while he drank from her wrist.

Unwilling to be forgotten, Max spread her ass cheeks, desperate to get more. He wrapped his lips around her clit and tugged, and sent Jesse crashing hard into a screaming orgasm.

"Yes, *sarasvatti.* I can't wait anymore, baby. I have to get inside you." Kit came to his knees on the ground, Max rolling out of his way, his chest lifting and falling like a bellow as he waited for what would happen next.

Kit kissed her open mouth, eating at her lips before turning her to face Max. He licked her wrist, leaning to whisper in her ear. "I'm going to take you, Jesse. Going to make you come again, while you show Max how good you are at sucking cock. Show him why I'm burning to fuck you, why your mouth drove me over the edge. This is all he can have of you, my angel. Just the feel of your hot mouth, the taste of you lingering on his tongue."

He lowered her to all fours. Max's large erection brushed her cheek, and Kit thrust inside her. "Ahhh!" So good. So full and hot and... "Yes, Kit. Yes!"

He pumped inside her, all pretence of gentleness gone. She loved it. Max moaned at the sight and Jesse turned her head, stroking his cock with her tongue.

"Shit." She smiled at his curse, opening her mouth to let him inside. This too was different. Just as big and overwhelming as Kit's, but Max tasted...different. Not bad, not better, just different. But she wanted to give back the ecstasy he'd given to her with his mouth and tongue. She wanted Max to come.

She relaxed her jaw, allowing Kit's powerful thrusts to push Max's cock deeper down her throat. Becoming mindless with the rhythm, mindless with sensation. Max caressed her hair gently, holding himself still for whatever she wanted to give, whatever he could have.

Her tongue dipped into the crevice on the head of his shaft, tasting the pearly dew of his pre-come, and he swore. Jesse smiled and sucked harder, determined to throw him over the edge with the rest of them.

"You see, Max? See why any man would kill to have those full lips wrapped around his cock? She's irresistable. I. Will. Never. Get. Enough." Kit punctuated his words with deep thrusts, so deep she could feel them to her soul. So deep she would never be able to be without him.

Max's fingers clenched in her curls, and she knew he was close. Knew Kit couldn't last much longer. She lowered her mouth as far as it could go, swallowing around the thick flesh while tightening the inner muscles of her sex around Kit.

Their shouts echoed across the ruins as they shared in their orgasms. Max pulled out, stroking himself as he came into his hand while Kit filled her with his climax. Jesse's head fell to the ground, loving the feel of the hot come dripping down her thighs. An unbidden wish, that she could have his child, a piece of him no matter what tomorrow might bring, flew into her mind.

She wasn't sure whose wish it was. Or if anyone would hear.

Kit lifted her, cradling her in his arms like a child. Soothing her with soft kisses and murmured words of love. Jesse blushed when her gaze clashed with Max's.

He stood and in a flash he was fully clothed. He bowed. "Thank you for honoring me, Miss Jesse. I will never forget the kindness." He met Kit's gaze. "And you, my cousin. I will leave you alone with your...mate, until the sun sets."

He headed through the crowd, giving them privacy. Jesse felt a moment's regret. Had it been a mistake? Would Kit's bond with his cousin be tainted by this? Would she ever be able to look him in the eye again?

"You are worrying, I can see it. If you say that wasn't enjoyable, I'll know you lie."

"It was. I just...I just feel..."

Kit kissed her forehead. "I know, angel. I never imagined I would be willing to share even that much with another. Even one I trust as much as I do Max. But I don't regret seeing your pleasure. And I don't regret sharing this memory with him. It will be he who must protect you when I'm gone."

Jesse pushed against his chest. "You're a bastard. Why can't we just cuddle after sex? No, you always have to remind me that I'm losing you. Well, here's a tip. Max is wonderful, but he isn't you. He will *never* be you. What he will be is a constant reminder of what I can't have. Of what Baal took from me. So don't even think of paving the way for Max and me to be together, because that will never happen."

Kit buried his face in her hair. "That shouldn't bring me joy, should it? For all my training I am just a selfish bastard, Jesse. I don't want you to find another. I just wanted to forget, for a while. Wanted to bring you as much joy as I could. I love you, *sarasvatti.* And even that is too weak a word. Not even death can conquer what I feel for you. What I'll always feel for you."

He kissed her neck, his voice cracking with a vulnerability he was unused to expressing. *"Sarasvatti."*

Jessed pulled him close, caressing his back with slow, soothing strokes. This wasn't fair. She sent a message upward. If her mother could hear her, if anyone could, she'd be willing to do whatever it took to change the course they were on. If Kit had to die, she didn't want to stay here without him. If she knew they'd be together...

What a mess.

Chapter Ten

"It's almost time, Miss Jesse."

She looked around, making sure no one was looking at her before Max touched her shoulder, causing her to disappear from their view. She'd taken a little time to walk among the other humans, giving Kit time to prepare for what was coming.

For the first time in a long time, she didn't envy the tourists their cameras. She was finally living in the present, on the other side of the lens. She didn't want to hide from it, she wanted to experience every last second. She'd found her life. And it was wonderful, and awful. But it was hers.

"Miss Jesse?"

She was blushing again. She wasn't sure how long it would take before she got over her embarrassment with Max. "You don't have to call me Miss, Max. Not after...you just don't, okay?"

Max stood a little taller. "It is even more important now. I use it to show respect. My mother would never forgive me if I showed the wife of my cousin anything less."

Jesse swallowed. “Wife? Did I miss something?”

“He has claimed you. Called you his mate, though our people have never been able to claim that deep a connection. And now, from what I can see, you two are linked just as surely as the Sariel Mediator and Miss Regina. As far as my people are concerned, you are bonded.”

Jesse rolled her eyes. “I’m sorry to break this to you, but *my* people require the man to ask, a white dress, family you *have* to invite and someone getting embarrassingly drunk at the reception before we consider ourselves officially husband and wife.” She looked away, lowering her voice. “And the honeymoon usually consists of two, not three participants.”

Max froze. “It was an honor I know I’m not worthy of, to be able to share in the love you feel for each other. And I know it’s not something that can ever be repeated. I only hope that someday I can find someone who loves me as completely as you love my cousin. It’s not a wish a Sariel guard should have, but it is one I cannot deny.”

Her heart melted, and she turned to throw herself into his arms. “You will, Max. You deserve it.” She sniffled and looked up at him, smiling when he wiped a tear from her eye. “So what did your father say would happen now?”

His expression grew somber. “The past will come alive. For all of us.”

“Max. Jesse. The sun sets. It’s time to enter the temple.”

Kit bent his head, kissing her so tenderly it brought more tears to her eyes. “Stay near Max, *sarasvatti.* Soon, this will be over, and I’ll have all night to hold you in my arms.”

Max placed his hand on her lower back, and the two of them followed Kit to the mammoth columns of Baal’s temple. When she’d taken the final step upon a well-worn patch of ground that no doubt used to be the floors of the sacred building, she heard a loud gong and then...

Magic.

She had seen the transformation of a man into a werewolf. She’d been on trial in front of actual giants who could have squashed her between their fingers like a grape. Hell, her entire adventure began because she’d been following a dream which turned out to be real. But what she saw happening around her was beyond description. Magic was the only word for it.

The people milling around disappeared as though they’d never existed. Loud sounds of creaking and groaning filled the air as columns rose from the ground, fitting together like gargantuan puzzle pieces, gleaming as though they’d just been carved and polished, smoothing out until they no longer looked Roman, they looked Igigian.

She glanced down at her feet, watching in awe as a colorful mosaic grew from the barren ground, spreading out to fill the newly forming temple. It was covered in artwork, similar to the style she had seen in the Halls of Record, but the stories they told were different. She saw the scorpion men from today's first challenge along with creatures straight out of a fairytale. A harpy and a gryffin were flying through the air, looking down upon a three-headed snake with what appeared to be a bloody mermaid in its central mouth.

Riding the monster was a man with the horns of a bull and the tongue of a snake. He wore a crown of lightning, carrying a bolt like a scepter in his hand. Baal. Jesse shuddered. Not exactly the serene and happy scenes one would imagine in a holy temple.

The inner walls that rose between each column were made of diamonds and gold, shimmering in the dimming light. A giant throne of onyx marble rose from the dirt, fully formed, while the braziers that had grown like branches from each column burst with flame to light their way. This was, indeed, a temple fit for the god of the giants.

"Who disturbs Baal's Temple? Come forward and speak your name."

Jesse jumped closer to Max at the sound of the booming voice. But her surprise turned to utter shock when a being stepped out from behind the mammoth throne.

"I am Kittim, son of Javan, warrior of the Igigi."

Max closed Jesse's jaw, but she barely noticed. She wanted to run screaming through the temple yelling, "Cyclops!" at the top of her lungs. Because as sure as she was standing there, that's what the man currently hobbling toward them was.

He stood taller than Max or Kit, his wrinkled face crowned by one large, ice blue eye in the middle of what should have been his forehead. He had no hair on his head, no eyelashes, and apart from the single eye, the rest of his features were decidedly average.

He turned his head, tilting it until she was worried he would lose his balance and fall completely over. "Of course, of course. Kittim. Guard of the Trueblood. Sorry about that mother of yours, yes? Yes. And Elam's son has come as a witness. Like father, like son."

The man took a large leaping step to land directly in front of Jesse. She couldn't stop the squeak that emerged when his large eye looked her up and down. "But who, who are *you*? I don't see you. I always see. It's what I do. Smell human. And something else? But what? What?"

He shook his head, scratching his chin before turning back toward Kit. "Makes no sense, but what can we do? Nothing, that's what. Must go on, lot to do."

Kit bowed. "It is an honor to meet you, Silas Who Waits. Our people recall your sacrifice with great admiration and reverence."

Silas cackled loudly. "Surely they do thank Silas Who Waits. And waits and waits alone for someone to come. For his people. His people who left long ago to hide in the mountains. But I still see, yes? Yes. Silas sees everything. Everything and everyone but the cute little maybe human. Can't see her. Ah, well. No time to visit. Never time to visit. I wait until you come, I show you what I see and then I wait again until another comes, yes? Yes."

Jesse bit her lip. That was the saddest thing she'd ever heard. Was he Igigi? Cyclops were giants, too, from what she could recall. Had they left him here alone? Or was Baal responsible?

She jerked when Silas focused on her once more. "Sad? For me? Ha! Must be human. Blessed God said his Mother made them soft. Too soft to survive. Fooled us all, yes? Yes. No more distractions, time to see. Time to face what must be faced."

The flames grew around them, light dancing on the jeweled walls, faster and faster until Jesse could have sworn she was in a dance club. Those places always made her dizzy. And she was dizzy. So unsteady she wasn't sure how much longer she could stand.

"Kit? Kit what's happening?"

"You're safe, angel. Let it come. It will be over soon."

Let what come? She put her hand to her head and heard it. Singing. It was her mother and Adrian. But how could that be? She dropped her hand and turned in a circle. "What the hell?"

"Jesse said a bad word! Jesse said a bad word!" An eight-year-old Adrian ran circles around her, giggling and pointing.

"Don't swear, Jesse. So impatient. But I know what you want. You better come and get it before the wax melts."

"Mom?" She walked through her childhood living room, pushing open the yellow kitchen door to where her mother stood, holding a cake in her hands.

"Happy birthday, my heart. Seven years old already. Time is going far too fast."

Her seventh birthday? What was she doing here? Had she fainted from the strobe lights?

"Jess, blow out the candles. Hurry up, I'm starving." Adrian went to stand next to their mother, trying to scoop a finger full of icing.

Jesse walked over in a daze and blew out her candles. She watched them cheer and head toward the plates, her mother slicing a piece for her impatient brother. She shook her head and plopped down in the nearest chair, utterly confused.

"I shouldn't be here. I should be with Kit. He needs my help."

"What, honey?" Her mother sat beside her with a smile, pushing a plate piled high with ice cream and a piece of chocolate cake in front of Jesse.

"I'm not hungry, Mom. But thanks. I just don't know why I'm here."

Her mother chuckled. "Well I've never lied to you, honey. Though I did think I had a few more years before we had to have this talk.You're here because when a man loves a woman—"

"Mom! Please stop. That isn't what I mean. It's just that this isn't a memory that seems particularly horrible." She patted her mother's hand. "You always made our birthdays special."

"Well thank you, honey. I'm a little confused, but I'll play along if you let me in on your game."

Jesse sighed. "I honestly don't know, Mom. I think that Cyclops just threw me into the wrong memory."

"Oh, you sound just like your father. He always told the most amazing stories. I used to ask him all the time to write them down. He even had one about a Cyclops named Silas, who gave up eternity and one of his eyes for the power to see the truth."

Jesse jumped from her chair, grabbing her mother's shoulders and pulling her up beside her. "*What?* Mom, did you say Silas? And *Dad* told you about him?"

She watched her mother nod, her eyes misting with memory, as they always did when she mentioned their father. "Yes. He always had such an amazing imagination. And when I was pregnant with you, he'd rub my feet and tell us stories every night. I miss those stories. I'm so glad you inherited his gifts."

Jesse's mind was racing. How could her father know? Did he share her ability to dream of the supernatural world? Is that where she got it from? Or was there another reason?

"Mom? Did Dad ever tell you where he was from?"

She shrugged. "He didn't like to talk about his past. Said he only wanted to live in the present, with us. But sometimes I'd find him outside at dusk, looking so melancholy that I knew he was thinking about another time and place." Her smile wobbled. "I thought I could be enough to make him happy."

Jesse hugged her, unable to see her mother sad. "I'm sorry, I really am. No one in his right mind would want to leave you, Mom. He was lucky to have you."

"He loved us, Jesse. You have to believe that. And he'll be back, whenever we really need him."

Jesse heard a strange note in her mother's voice and pulled away. "Did he say that?"

Adrian zoomed past on a sugar high and her mother followed him with her gaze, all smiles again. "He said it all the time. And the first night you came home from the hospital, he held you in his arms and sat beside me while I was feeding Adrian. He had a very serious look on his face. He promised that if we ever needed him, if we were ever in trouble, he would be there. We just had to call on him. And trust our hearts."

Jesse felt her heart sink. "But he never came, Mom. No matter how many times I wished he would. And when you got sick, I wished every day."

Her mother cupped her cheek. "You made those wishes for me, dear, not for yourself. *You* never needed him. Not really. Not like you do now."

"What?"

"Trust your heart, Jesse. That's all you have to do."

A wave of dizziness hit her, so strong it knocked her to the floor. She closed her eyes, trying to calm her racing heart. When she opened them again, one large, ice blue eye filled her vision.

Silas cackled when she scrambled away from him. "First one back. I'm surprised. Not easy to surprise me, right? Right. I can see everything. But not you. Why? Tell Silas."

"I-I don't know. I swear."

He waved his hand, swatting at her words. "Doesn't matter. Funny, yes? Yes. I gave up all to see. Now I would give up all to see nothing. Tired, tired, tired. Tired of knowing. Always knowing who will die. Kittim, Javan, all of them. Tired of knowing. Tired of showing them the worst parts."

Jesse got to her knees, seeing Kit and Max lying on the tiles, seeing the walls cracking. But she couldn't worry about that yet. "Silas, tell me. Did you see Kit die?"

He backed up the steps to the large onyx throne, before sitting with a thud that shook the room. He looked shattered. "I see everyone die. Die, die, die. All I wanted was to help my people, to help my family. And all I see is death. How does that help anyone? It helps nothing. Poor Silas, yes? Yes."

The throne began to sink. "Wait, Silas, please. *Silas!*" He lowered his head, covering his ears and sobbing as the earth swallowed him whole. The temple began to quake, shards of marble crumbling to the ground.

Jesse ran to the two warriors, throwing her body over them to protect them from the shrapnel. She closed her eyes, heedless of her tears. She cried for Silas. For her mother. They'd both acted out of love, and they'd both been abandoned.

Maybe she was crying for herself as well. Tomorrow she would join their ranks.

Jesse had been silent since they left Baalbek. He'd tried his damnedest to reach her through their link, but either she was blocking him or he didn't have the ability to open their connection.

He should be glad. He didn't want to talk about what he'd seen during the second challenge. The truths he'd had to face about himself, about his family. Even Max looked shaken.

When they'd come to, Jesse had been plastered against them, crying like an inconsolable child. It had broken his heart to see her like that. But she wouldn't take his compassion. She'd just wiped her cheeks and lifted her chin, asking them what came next.

They'd decided they had time to take her into town and get a room with running water and food. They took care of her as though she were fragile, and indeed she seemed to be. Max even turned on the television to a music video station, thinking human sounds would calm her. But it was something they called "Oldies Hour" and she heard a song that made her throw a shoe at the irritating box, so they turned it off again.

It was late when they set out for their final destination. Dawn would soon be approaching, and they were almost there—the mountains of Lebanon, where the Igigi were first set upon the Earth by their creator. The first of his kind had lived in a cave at the highest peak, and that was where Kit knew they had to go for the final ritual.

This was wrong. It went against his DNA to just lie down and submit. And the closer he got, the harder it was to take another step. Especially with Jesse in his arms. All too soon he'd leave her and Max at the mouth of the cave, and go to face his fate alone. There was no honor in this.

He could only pray to Great Mother that the people he loved would be safe when he was gone. Jesse, the Sariels, little Alexei. They all deserved happiness. All deserved to live. And in the end, they were his only reason for pressing forward. Not duty after all. Family.

"Do you feel that?"

Kit nodded at Max, all his senses on alert. There was movement up ahead. He counted five separate heartbeats. His own started to pound furiously when he recognized their scents. He spoke loudly in the darkness. "Max? Could you hold Jesse for a minute? I have to beat a few Were and Trueblood heads together."

"Hello to you too. Would you believe, we were just passing through?"

Lux smiled as he appeared in their path, an expression of *faux* innocence gracing his features. His brother, Zander came up behind him, shrugging in apology. "We took a wrong turn. We were actually headed toward Paris for this great club we heard about, but you know Truebloods have absolutely no sense of direction."

Kit bit the inside of his cheek when Regina's golden gaze peered out from between the two, taller men. He felt his fangs extend when Glynn Magriel popped up beside her. Regina's smile was wobbly. "The truth is, we heard a few of our dearest friends were about to head into danger all alone. And we couldn't let that happen."

"Where are your Sariel guards?" Kit raised one eyebrow at Max's question, wondering the answer to that himself.

Regina blushed, but Zander answered. "We sent them away. Along with a message of rebuke to your Old Ones for threatening a relative of the Sariels and an innocent human. Not to mention taking two of our best trained warriors from our midst."

"Bet they'll be thrilled to hear that. They seemed like a really relaxed group of giants."

"Jasyn!" Kit nearly dropped Jesse in surprise as she recognized the Beta. He let her squirming body down, frowning severely as she made a beeline straight toward the bastard.

Jasyn opened his arms to greet her, the huge grin on his face warping into a grimace as she punched him hard in the stomach. "Do you know how much trouble you nearly got us into? Do you have that darn stone? And where the hell is my camera bag?"

"I knew I liked her." Lux went to stand beside Kit, watching the crowd erupt in laughter. "She has spunk."

"Ouch. What did you do that for?" Jesse watched Jasyn rub his midsection with a certain amount of satisfaction.

"You left me there, alone, with giants who'd just as soon eat me as let me go. I think that deserves a knuckle sandwich or two."

Jasyn winked. "That depends on what you mean by eat. Hey!" He held up his hands as she raised her fist again. "I'm sorry but She told me to. And you shouldn't turn down the Mother. I think that's some kind of law."

"*The* Mother? Or *my* mother?"

"Huh?"

Jesse suddenly realized she was playing to an audience. Her cheeks heated as she turned to face the small party watching her with rapt fascination. A part of her was happy to see them, happy that they'd come to show Kit their support. But her emotions were so close to the surface, so fragile she felt like she was going to snap in two at any moment.

Regina and Glynn came over and wrapped her in a warm, female embrace. The priestess whispered in her ear. "Jasyn told us about Kit. Don't lose hope, young Jesse. Trust me. Better yet, trust your heart."

Jesse lifted her head, her brow wrinkling at Priestess Magriel's words. What was going on? Hadn't her mother said the same thing? What did it mean? How could she trust anymore than she was? Hadn't she followed her heart halfway across the world? Wasn't she standing by Kit, even as they came closer and closer to a situation that was fraught with heartache and suffering?

The women released her to stand in front of Jasyn, protecting him from the snarling Max. "There is a price on your head, Beta. My people have your scent, and they won't rest until you are brought to justice for what you stole."

Jesse stepped forward, placing a hand on Max's chest. "Listen to him first, Max."

Max blinked, his lips lowering over his fangs as he stared at Jesse. Without taking his eyes from hers, he spoke again. "Speak, Dydarren."

"I can't." All the women looked at him in disbelief, and Jasyn raised his hands as if to ward them off. "I'm following orders. What I have to say I can only say to Jesse, and only when the time is right. That's what She said."

"The Mother?" Kit stood beside Max, his face expressionless. "The Mother told you to steal Legacy from my people?"

"I didn't steal it, damn it. I know I'm not the *Antara*, not anything special. But the Great Mother came to me in a dream, and I couldn't deny her request. I think anyone here would have done the same."

"Of course we would have." Lux stood with the women at Jasyn's side. "We've trusted our Goddess, and she has never let us down."

Max was shaking his head. "She wouldn't interfere with this. It's forbidden."

"I'm not sure anything is forbidden to the mother of the gods, Max. Especially when all her children, Were, Vampire, Giant and...human, are united in asking for her help." Zander smiled warmly at Jesse, joining the protective circle surrounding Arygon's brother.

"It's okay, Max. You and I both know Great Mother has an eye on Jesse. Unexplainable things keep happening around her. You'll take the stone when this is through, and tell Master Elam about the request of our Goddess. He'll make the Old Ones understand." Kit pulled Jesse into his arms, lifting her until their lips were level, and kissed her.

Her toes curled. She loved the feel of his lips on hers. She breathed deep, pulling his scent into her lungs, desperate to memorize every sensation, every texture. He lifted his lips until they brushed across the tops of hers. "Just felt like claiming you again. I'm not sure what it is about you, angel. You bring out the jealous beast in me."

"I love you."

"And I love you, sarasvatti. *Forever."*

"Kit." They looked over at Max, his gaze on the horizon again. The sky was changing, lightening, though the sun was still hidden from view. Oh God. Her eyes welled up. This couldn't be the end. It couldn't.

Kit set her down but didn't release her, holding her tightly against him while he spoke to the somber crowd. "Thank you. All of you. It means more to me than I can express, that you all cared enough to come here. I'll never forget it. Max, guard them well, my cousin." He turned, with her still beside him, and continued down the path.

"Oh, I don't think so." Regina appeared in front of them, hands on her hips, dark hair flying behind her.

"You can't just leave us here and go off like a good soldier to accept your fate."

Jesse knew she loved Regina. "That's what I've been telling him."

"If I deny Baal, he will flood the world with his anger. Alexei, Sylvain's twins...all will die. I cannot let that happen. I must enter our place of beginnings when the first ray of sunlight reaches the cave."

"But there's no rule that says you have to go alone."

"Max?" Jesse nearly swallowed her tongue. Dudley Do-Right was agreeing with Regina?

Max smiled sadly at Jesse. "My father told me long ago of the choice he'd had to make. He was determined to follow Javan, Kit. Into the bowels of Hell and back if he had to. But your father talked him out of it. Javan reminded him of his duty to me, to the warriors, and to the Igigi people, to prepare the next of us for the challenge."

He looked Kit directly in the eye. "When we left the settlement, my father told me he'd made the wrong choice. I will not do the same. I'll stand beside you to the end. Be a true witness."

"We're all going. You may as well give in, Kit old boy. The Mother's child wants his vengeance? Well, he'll have to go through us to do it." Lux rubbed his hands together, as though looking forward to the coming battle.

"You've been married to the *Antara* too long, Sariel. You think you're invincible." Kit shook his head. "I don't have time to argue. I have to go."

"Kit, I've been dreaming about you and these people most of my life. I have a feeling they aren't going to take no for an answer."

"Angel—"

"And neither will I."

Jesse crossed her arms, looking at him, determination in her gaze. She knew the moment he gave in. "You win, *sarasvatti.* You all win. Just promise to stay behind me. And do not speak. He is easily angered. I would never forgive myself if any of you are hurt because of me."

Kit started walking, head shaking as though he couldn't quite believe this turn of events. Max and Zander followed close behind, with Lux, Jasyn and the women bringing up the rear.

"How is it that you can link with Kit telepathically? That was what all that silent staring stuff was about right? I thought he said it wasn't possible. That his people didn't mate." Jasyn lowered his voice, shifting something around beneath his jacket so he could bend closer.

"Your guess is as good as mine. Now I have a question for you. What was all that nonsense about the goddess having something to say to me? In the dream I remember you talking to my very normal, human mother, and her trying to play Cupid with you and Hannah. I don't remember *The* Mother being anywhere around the place."

"It's not nonsense, Jesse. You'll see."

She glared at Jasyn. "Well I better see pretty damn soon, Jasyn Dydarren. It's not like we have that much more time. If anyone is playing their aces close to the vest, they should show their hand before the man of my dreams is killed on the altar of Baal's ego."

"Sorry to interrupt, but Sylvain wanted me to tell you she is with you in spirit. Unfortunately the twins decided that they didn't want to miss out on any excitement either, and she had to return home to keep Arygon from going mad."

"Oh, they came." Jesse smiled at Lux over her shoulder, momentarily distracted by the happy news. "It's strange not instantly knowing what's going on in all your lives. I'm so used to the dreams. But now..." She shrugged.

"Now you are a part of it. A part of us. Who knows? Maybe another is dreaming of all this right now." Glynn Magriel winked, her swirl of tattoos becoming visible in the growing light.

The light. It had grown light enough to see everything. The sun would be visible any minute. She was beginning to hate the sun. Regina gasped. "Jesse. Look."

They'd stepped out onto a rise, the view stretching out for miles. Beneath them was a sight she hadn't expected. A mountain oasis. A pool of brilliant blue water, a patch of emerald green grass, fruit trees and palms for shade. And the entrance to a cave. *The* cave. She saw Kit and Max kneeling off to the side, their sword tips in the dirt, their heads bowed over their hilts in prayer.

Zander motioned to the rest of them, and they headed down the slight slope. Jesse lagged behind. What was the answer? There had to be a way to save Kit *and* the world.

Surely their Great Mother wouldn't want this to continue. She couldn't.

"It's time, Jesse. Those were Great Mother's words. She said, 'When the moment is perilous, and the time draws near, Jesse will hold all life in her hands and trust her heart.'" Jasyn pulled her camera bag out from beneath his jacket, handing it to her quickly before joining the others at the cave's entrance.

Hold all life in her hands? Jesse looked inside the heavy bag, knowing her camera wasn't there. It was the opalescent stone. The Legacy. The gift to the Igigi that had been guarded since the flood. What on Earth was *she* supposed to do with it? She didn't even know what it was. Or why it was suddenly glowing.

Kit stood, looking for her over the throng as the sun's first light started to glimmer on the horizon. He took a step toward her, confusion in his eyes as he looked above and around her. Her jaw dropped. He couldn't see her. Jesse looked at the stone again. How could he not see her?

There was no more time, and Jesse knew it. He swore, turning to enter the mouth of the cave, the others close behind him. Jesse ran to catch up, stumbling a bit with the heavy stone cradled carefully in her arms.

She entered the cave right behind Jasyn. "Are you sure about the message, Jasyn? Sure it was meant for me?"

He didn't answer, didn't even turn in her direction. She pushed past him, coming up alongside a worried

Regina. "Can you read anything from inside? If you could hear what Baal was thinking..."

No response.

"Damn it, why isn't anyone listening to me? Am I invisible or something?" Silence. "Holy shit, I'm invisible. But how can I help if he doesn't even know I'm here?"

They reached a large hollowed out cavern. There were crude drawings on the rock walls, a fire pit already lit and an altar just beyond it.

The group fanned out against the walls while Kit stood boldly in the center, before the fire. He turned to look at them, his jaw tense with worry as he sought out another face.

"I'm here, Kit! I'm right here, dammit!" She set down the stone, which had been glowing brighter with each passing moment. "Can you see me now?"

No one turned. No one heard. Thunder rumbled inside the cavern and lightning struck the fire. Kit didn't even flinch as a man appeared before him. A man with short ebony hair, blindingly beautiful. Just as tall and broad as any Igigi.

Baal.

Chapter Eleven

From the shadows two grotesque creatures hopped on jagged claws toward the man, their wings flapping in their excitement as they came to stand beside him. He stroked the horrid beasts, cooing at them as though they were cute little parakeets. Jesse gagged.

"Javan's son. My pets tell me you brought a little human with you, but all I see are flea traps and blood suckers. Did she run home? Too bad. I was looking forward to meeting her. Humans are...delicious...don't you agree?"

Jesse's jaw dropped. Wait a minute. Baal couldn't see her either? What kind of god was he? The Legacy stone seemed to be pulsing, calling to her. It had to mean something. She bent to pick it up.

"Unfortunately, you'll have to settle for me. Did you get my message?"

Baal chuckled harshly. "But I don't have to settle for you, Kittim. You've brought friends to the party. Were they so anxious to watch you die for your God?"

"We are Great Mother's children. Not yours."

Baal stepped forward into the flames, his voice thunderous as it bounced off the rock. "*I* made you. *I* created you. You exist at *my* whim. You can burn my mark from your body, sing praises to my Mother night and day. You can even protect her little pets. But *I* am your God. If you don't believe me, just ask Maximus."

Jesse turned at Lux's shout. Max had fallen to the ground in a heap, his eyes open but lifeless. "Max! No. No. No. *No*."

"Coward," Kit spat the word in Baal's face, his expression enraged. "*I* was chosen for your sacrifice. Not Max. You break the law."

"I am the law. Don't worry, your turn will come. But it's hard to resist these kinds of offerings. Mate of the *Antara*, the last Reader, you even brought a priestess."

He glanced at Jasyn and Zander. "Doesn't it ever bother you that my dear sainted Mother bestows her best gifts on the females? Talk about favoritism." He looked up as though talking to the heavens. "You have to have a damn uterus to get her attention these days."

Baal shrugged, smiling once more. "She won't stop me though. She can't. Not here. This is my sacred ground. My sacrifice. But, I doubt she'll be pleased when I do this."

Jesse's mouth opened on a soundless scream when one by one, they all fell to land beside Max. Regina, Glynn, Lux. Everyone. Jesse fell to her knees. What was she supposed to do? How could she possibly stop a god?

Trust your heart.

They'd all said it. Even her mother. What had her mother been talking about? She'd said her father would come if he needed her, really needed her. She only had to trust her heart. "Great Mother, I don't know if you can hear me. I don't know if anyone can hear me. I need help. Daddy? Daddy please help me. I need you."

Her sobs became gasps of disbelief as the knowledge began pouring into her through the stone. Between one breath and the next she knew. She knew what she had to do.

"Kit?"

"Jesse? Thank the Goddess. Wherever you are stay away, angel. He's killed everyone. Even...Max. I can't let him get away with it anymore. Remember that I love you." She watched him raise his sword at the laughing Baal.

"No! Wait, Kit. Pull him into that shadow space. The space where time slows. Don't think about it, just do it. Trust me."

He didn't hesitate. He leapt into the fire, wrapping his arms around the shrieking Baal, and in moments everything changed. Jesse looked around. The cave around them looked the same, just gray and grainy. And the beasts that had been standing beside Baal were moving around in slow motion panic. Strange.

"What is this place? I was there when the Earth was created, but I don't recognize this."

Kit sneered at Baal. "This is my world, Baal. Welcome." Kit pulled back his fist and let it fly, throwing the stunned god across the floor and into the altar.

"You lose your powers here, but you don't really need those, do you, Baal?" He kicked the deity in his side, pulling him up by the scruff of his shirt to pound his fist into Baal's nose, smiling at the crunching sound. "Or maybe *you* do."

"Kit. Not that I'm not enjoying this, but we don't know how long this space will stay open."

"Jesse?"

"I'm here, love. I'm here. And so is—"

"Shalem! I should have known you'd be behind this." Baal spat blood, pushing away from Kit and stumbling toward the blond man behind him.

"You give me too much credit, brother. I could not have done this without the entire family behind me. And Jesse of course. She opened the portal with her heartfelt request, and we saw everything. Including you, breaking your own laws of sacrifice." Shalem winked at Jesse, holding out his hands for the Legacy stone.

Jesse could hardly see through her tears as she handed it over gratefully, running to Kit's ready embrace.

"You lie. The sacrifice is mine by right. Not even our Mother can interfere. I must have satisfaction."

Shalem shook his head. "You are so full of hate, Baal Hadad. You always have been. But your time has come and gone. You are forgotten. And so you must remain." He rubbed the glimmering stone, whispering in a language that sounded like music to Jesse's ears.

A brilliant flash of light erupted from the stone and engulfed the bitterly cursing god. When Shalem turned to face Kit and Jesse, the stone and Baal had both disappeared, and they were no longer in the shadow space.

"What just happened?" Jesse watched as the angelic being touched Baal's creatures with the tips of his fingers, transforming them into beautiful falcons, who squawked gratefully before flying toward the cave's exit.

"He's been imprisoned for his crimes against creation. As a child of the Mother and Father, he cannot be killed. But he will remain in the space between, buried and under guard for eternity."

"What if he escapes?" Kit had that Sariel guard expression on his face again, that one she couldn't read. Wasn't he happy to be alive?

Shalem just smiled. "The Mother herself begs me to assure you that your people are free. There will be no more chosen, no more *mahan calati.* The sacrifice and compassion of Max, Jesse and the others gave her what she needed to break the laws that bound us."

He caught Jesse's gaze. "You did well. Your mother and I were sure you would."

Jesse left the safety of Kit's arms and ran to embrace Shalem. "Thank you for coming."

"Thank you for finally needing me." She felt him look over her head toward Kit. "Take care of this young lady. She's special."

"I know. And I will. You have my vow."

Jesse smiled into Shalem's shoulder, pulling back with a shriek when she remembered.

"What about Max and Jasyn and everyone? He killed them. And Silas. What will happen to Silas?"

Shalem chuckled, kissing her forehead before stepping out of her embrace, his palms splayed. "You have your mother's heart, Jesse. Do not fear. Your friends wake even as we speak. As for Silas, he has suffered enough. He will have a place with us, where he can choose to see or not, as he pleases."

Kit knelt on the hard floor of the cavern. "My people will honor your name for all time for this."

Shalem shook his head as he began to fade from view. "Honor our Mother, you are *her* children after all. And honor and keep Jesse for as long as you both shall live. Which might be longer than she thinks." With another wink, he was gone.

"What the hell just happened? My brain feels like it's been liquefied." Jasyn rubbed his neck, groaning, while the others began to clamber to their feet.

"Nothing exciting." Jesse looked up at Kit, who seemed to be realizing for the first time that he wouldn't have to sacrifice his life for his people, and grinned damply. "Baal is gone, the world is saved and I...I just met my father."

"Don't be silly."

"How am I being silly? A Sariel guard is never silly. It's trained completely out of us before we can hold a sword."

"Blah. Blah. Blah. I hear you talking, but I still say you're silly to be nervous."

Jesse bit her lip to hold back the giggles desperately trying to escape. He'd been a wreck for hours. The closer she came to being ready to go, the more ridiculous he became. "It's just a wedding."

He came up behind her as she put in her earrings. She watched his expression in the mirror's reflection, still a little in awe of how much she loved him. She finally understood why her mother had waited. If she loved Shalem half as much as Jesse loved Kit, it made perfect sense.

"It's *our* wedding, *sarasvatti*, and well you know it. It's not *that* that I'm nervous about. It's that your father, the God of Twilight, may decide I don't deserve you, and send me into the Underworld to scrub toilets for the next thousand years."

Jesse laughed. "My mother would never let it happen. Neither would Meredith. I think my sister-in-law has a crush on you."

Her brother Adrian had a harder time accepting the truth. He'd loved mythology, so the magical parts of her adventure had fascinated him. And learning that he was not entirely human certainly did wonders for his ego, and no doubt drove Meredith crazy. But to find out that their father had left them to ensure their protection from Baal was a hard pill to swallow. Especially for a son who'd spent a lifetime feeling abandoned.

Jesse hadn't told him his other reason, that he'd gone to keep Jesse off the radar until she was old enough to follow her destiny. A destiny the Mother had planned for her. It was heady stuff. She'd spent her whole life thinking she was average. Now she was marrying a giant who was thousands of years old, and being given away by her father, the god. It was a lot for anyone to take in.

She'd gotten to talk with him on a regular basis in her dreams. Shalem had let her rant and question his love for her mother. Let her demand to know where he was while she was dying of cancer. Why he couldn't just save her before she'd had to go through all that pain.

"I was being watched, daughter. My brother knew something happened to me on my visit to Earth. He has spies everywhere. If I'd shown favoritism while she was still alive, you all would have died."

Jesse had seen the tears escaping down his cheeks and knew he was sincere. "I've tried to make up for all she's suffered since she joined me here. But I know an eternity will not suffice for what we've all lost because of my weakness, and my brother's jealousy. I only hope you and your brother will give me a chance to try."

Jesse was willing. Adrian would just take a little patience.

Kit's people had been overjoyed to hear the story of all that had transpired. Well, most of them. Max and Elam had both arrived at the Haven Pub, determined to fulfill Javan's oath, regardless of the current chaos and power transitions occurring among the Old Ones.

The last Jesse had heard, Kit's mother had been kicked off the council, and she and Kaine had disappeared from the settlement. All she could say to that was good riddance. The last thing she'd wanted was to invite her giant witch of a mother-in-law to her nuptials. But Kit was worried. He was sure they wouldn't stay out of trouble for long.

The Truebloods and Weres had been abuzz with excitement at Kit and Jesse's wedding plans. He was doing it for her, she knew. She was half human, she'd been raised human, and damn it, she wanted a human wedding. And, it seemed, everyone wanted to help.

Zander and Regina had not only helped plan everything, offering Haven as wedding central, but they'd been kind enough to put them up in Lux's old rooms for a while. Apparently Nicolette had found new "sleeping arrangements" with one of the most prestigious members of the Clan Trust.

Lux had made them promise to visit Dydarren lands after the honeymoon, since Sylvain and Arygon were both still pouting from being left out of the last adventure. But there were no true hard feelings. Sylvain had even offered to do the flowers for her wedding. And when the *Antara* was the florist, well, Jesse had a feeling everything was going to be perfect.

She couldn't wait to see everyone. Even Jasyn was coming. She had so much to thank him for. Maybe her mother's new matchmaking scheme would work. Only time would tell.

She heard the familiar click and whir of her camera and turned to find Kit aiming it directly at her butt. She stalked him. "What do you think you're going to do with those, you big galoot?"

"Meredith said she'd make me something called a Book Face page."

"*Facebook*? Oh no you don't.My butt isn't going to be plastered all over the web just because you've found a new toy." He let her tackle him, rolling with her on the bed until she was underneath him.

"Okay. But I want something in return, my little human goddess."

She narrowed her eyes. "What?"

He whispered in her ear and she blushed. "*Now?*"

Kit sat up on the edge of the bed, his feet firmly planted on the floor before he reached for her. "Right now. You've been a bad girl, *sarasvatti.* And bad girls need to be punished."

She couldn't contain her shriek of delight when he slid her over his lap, white dress and all. "What about our wedding?"

He raised his palm high. "We'll be late. It's not as though they can start without us, angel."

How could she argue with logic like that? "Don't you dare wrinkle my dress."

Kit chuckled. "Trust me, *sarasvatti.*"

Her dress disappeared and Jesse covered her instant arousal with a laugh. "At least you'll never expect me to do your dirty laundry."

"There are many things I expect of my new bride." He lowered his hand on her left ass cheek with a satisfying smack. "I expect her to crave my touch." Her right cheek got the same treatment, and Jesse pushed herself into his hands, loving the tingles that spread down her legs and into her sex at his firm touch.

"I crave your touch."

He purred, spreading her red cheeks to press his thumb teasingly against her there, where he'd given her more pleasure than she'd ever imagined.

"I expect her to love the feel of my cock, my fingers, my *tongue* inside her. Everywhere." He bent over her, lifting her hips to spear her ass with his tongue.

"Oh God. I love it. I do—I... *Oh God.*"

Kit smiled against her skin, his tongue circling the tight muscles, until she was trembling, her blood heating with need. "Kit, please."

His thumb pressed deeper, around his tongue, pushing inside and making her shout in pleasure. All thoughts of wedding plans and family left her head. All she could think of was him inside her, anyway he wanted, as long as he wanted. She opened her mind, sharing her thoughts with him.

He groaned, flipping her onto the bed and sliding in between her thighs. "You drive me crazy. I love it when you do that. Love to feel you inside my head. In me."

"I love it too. Mate."

"You are my mate, aren't you, sweet sarasvatti*? You claimed me long ago, and now I'm claiming you."*

Kit opened his mouth over her breast, sucking hard, the way she loved it. Piercing her skin with his fangs. She let his emotions wash over her. The heat and hunger. The adoration. The love. And she gave him hers in return.

She wrapped her legs around his waist, welcoming him inside her body. His strong arms took most of his weight, hips gentle against hers as he thrust inside her. Yes. She loved how big he was, how tightly he filled her sex with his cock.

"If you don't stop projecting I won't be able to hold back, baby."

"If you don't stop holding back your almost wife will scream."

Kit lifted his mouth from her breast and growled. "You want to see an Igigi without control? Want to see why we hold back?"

Jesse opened her mouth on an airless gasp as she felt it. Holy Mother in heaven it was growing. His cock was growing inside her. He'd been massive before, but now...now no amount of biting could relax her sex enough. She was stretched to capacity. Pain and pleasure. She tightened around him.

"Fuck. Jesse, *yes.* I can't move, baby. Do that again. *Fuck me.* Fuck me, angel." Kit arched his neck, baring his bloodied fangs as she complied, rhythmically tightening and releasing her internal muscles around his enormous shaft.

She watched his chest heave with the power of his arousal, his cheeks ruddy, eyes completely black as she massaged his cock with her pussy. It was so intensely intimate, their bodies still, all their attention focused on that one spot where they were joined.

He slipped two fingers between them, squeezing her clit gently in time to her clenching sex. "Ah."

"Yes, angel. Come for me. I can't wait, Jesse. I can't wait anymore."

Neither could she. It was too much. Too good. She joined her mind with his completely. Her climax was stunning in its power. She cried out his name and he shouted in reply, his hot seed exploding from his shaft with enough force to send her hurtling over the edge on another wave of pleasure.

"Mine. You are mine, sarasvatti. *Only mine. Forever."*

"And you are mine."

"I'm so glad you asked your father to do this, honey. He loves you so much."

Jesse smiled at her mother through her tears. She never imagined that she'd be able to marry the man of her dreams, but even more impossible was the idea that her mother would be a part of her special day. "I'm glad too, Mom."

"I told you nothing on Earth could stop the sacrifice. But it took *you* to open the portal, to take the leap of faith that allowed the plan to be realized. I told you that you were special." Her mother adjusted the small, tea roses that had been strategically tangled in Jesse's auburn locks. "The Mother only knows how hard it's been for me to stay away from you and Adrian all this time. But it was the only way. All I ever wanted was your happiness."

Jesse took her mother's trembling hand, kissing her cheek. "I understand, Mom, I really do."

"No you don't." Her father walked in, dressed in a silver coat buttoned up to his neck. His blond, youthful good looks were stunning to behold. Her mother blushed when he winked at her. "But you will when you have children of your own."

A small cloud crossed over Jesse's heart. She and Kit had both come to terms with the fact that they could never have children. But that wasn't something she wanted to think about today.

"Ready, Jesse?" Shalem held out his arm and she hugged her mother, placing her hand on his jacket.

"Ready."

They stepped outside, into the dark night, and Jesse sighed. The moon was full and bright, shining on a scene right out of a fairytale. There were green vines and flowers everywhere, petals strewn along the cobblestone street that was acting as a makeshift aisle.

Brilliant white roses formed a bower at the end of the aisle. She saw Glynn Magriel in her blue robe, smiling serenely as she waited to perform the ceremony. And there, beside her, stood Kit, looking uncomfortable in his tailor-made suit, but happy.

"You're wrong you know."

Jesse turned her head to study her father's pale eyes. "Wrong about what?"

"You forget that you're only half human, my daughter. The other half of you is of the gods. That changes our Mother's rules a bit. Think about it."

He started to walk her up the aisle, leaving her to sort through his confusing declaration in silence. What did he mean? Her mind flashed back to the conversation with her mother, and she stumbled.

Shalem's arm tightened, helping her regain her balance, and he grinned, knowing that she'd figured it out.

"Kit?"

"Are you okay, sarasvatti? *Your father is walking too slow for my taste. I find I'm impatient to claim you in every way there is."*

She shook her head, her smile beaming as she finally arrived beside him. He took her hand and she stepped in closer. She placed his knuckles against her silk-covered belly and opened her mind to his.

As Priestess Magriel began to speak of eternal love and unity, Jesse watched Kit's dark eyes grow damp.

"Truly?"

"I know. I can't believe it either."

"I can believe it, sarasvatti. *You found me, you saved me, and you gave me something I never thought a Sariel guard could have. Love. Anything is possible, as long as I have my guardian angel beside me."*

Jesse didn't hear most of the ceremony, could hardly recall the party that followed, or her mother's whispered asides about her schemes for Jasyn and Hannah. Her heart was too full. Her happiness too overwhelming. What did you do when all your dreams came true?

It looked like she was going to find out.

About the Author

Stolen away by a free-spirited Gypsy as a child (though she still swears she's my mother), I spent my childhood roaming the countryside, meeting fascinating characters and having amazing adventures. As the perpetual "new kid", my friends more often than not were found between the pages of a book...and in my own imagination. I read everything I could get my hands on. At the age of 11, I read my first romance and I've been hooked ever since.

I've been a nurse, a lead vocalist in several bands, a published lyricist and even a returning university student majoring in Anthropology and Mythology. Throughout all of my varied careers, I would sigh as I read one fantasy-filled story after another saying, "Someday I want to write one of those", until one day my husband said, "So do it." And I did. Now I can't imagine doing anything else.

To learn more about R. G. Alexander please visit www.rgalexander.com. Send an email to R. G. Alexander at r.g.alexander@hotmail.com.

What Happens When a Wicked Wizard Woos a Wary Witch?

Surrender Dorothy

© 2009 R.G. Alexander

Sequel to Not in Kansas

Dorothy knows her new neighbor is too wicked to be trusted. As a natural witch, she recognizes the Wizard for what he truly is. As a woman, she recognizes him as a threat to her sanity.

Z has tried everything. Pursued her in dreams, bribed her cat, enticed her with peep shows meant to whet her appetite and drive her crazy. And still she resists. What's a Wizard to do? He came to Earth to have an adventure, not lose his heart to the one witch whose guard he can't get past.

When he finally gets his hands on her, the power between them is undeniable. But Dorothy's family secret could make him sorry she surrendered.

Warning: Voyeurism, lurid dreams, raunchy dirty wizard sex in public places.

Available now in ebook from Samhain Publishing.

Enjoy the following excerpt from Surrender Dorothy...

He stood away from the wall, his fingers reaching up to undo the top button of his white linen shirt. Dorothy took a step back. "What are you doing?"

He took another step. "Earning your trust." Another button undone. "I never had any interest in Emily. She was merely a way for me to get close to you. I never touched her."

Dorothy bumped against a piece of furniture, altering her retreat without looking where she was going. "You're interested in everyone. You forget I had a bird's eye view of just how interested. Why should I believe you?"

He slipped the shirt off, and it dropped to the ground. Dorothy swallowed. He was beautiful. The ruby amulet lay against his lean, smooth chest, stomach muscles rippling with his slow, deliberate movements as he continued to stalk her. "I was never intimate with any of them, not after seeing you, and you know it. I wanted you to know me. To know my appetites. To want me not in spite of them,"—he smiled—"but because of them. And don't lie and say you didn't enjoy every minute of it."

She had. Dorothy heard the rushing of water and she looked behind her. He'd backed her into a room with a small waterfall. Steam rose from the heated pool at its base. This was a bathroom a woman could die happy in. But first she had to know.

"And Kansas?"

"He was fated to be the king's consort. The magic of our world called him, but yes, I sent the storm. Yes, I was attracted to him. And yes, I slept with him. That *is* what you wanted to know, isn't it?"

The waterfall blurred before her eyes. "Yes."

"Look at me, Dorothy. Please."

He was naked. Gloriously, unashamedly naked, aroused and looking at her as if she were the only thing he wanted in the universe. If only she could believe that.

He held out his arms. "I stand here before you, Zenamulous of the Crow Warriors, the king's wizard, from a line of wizards dating back to the time of Transformation. I have never used my magic to increase my wealth or power, though occasionally I have used it to increase another's pleasure. I have never repressed my passions, but I've never forced them on anyone either."

His chin lifted proudly, but Dorothy could see a hint of vulnerability darken his gaze. "And from the moment I saw you, I knew you were mine."

The ball was in her court. She could see it in the way he held himself so still. He wouldn't use words or powers to woo her, wouldn't take her in his arms or sweep her off her feet. She would have to make the next move. She would have to choose to trust him...or not.

In spite of her pique, in spite of her insecurities and his past, the choice wasn't hard at all. Hadn't she ridden a storm to find him? A few steps were nothing after that. She stopped directly in front of him, making sure he had a clear view. One twist of her fingers and the blanket fell silently to the floor.

His fiery stare scorched her skin. There could be no doubt he liked what he saw. His nostrils flared when she laid one tentative hand on his bare shoulder, skimming it down his arm to wrap around his wrist. He raised his eyebrow and she smiled, lifting his hand and covering it as it cupped her breast.

Dorothy closed her eyes, reveling in the feel of his hand on her. "Oh none of that." Her lids lifted, startled at Z's low command. "I want you to see everything. To look in your eyes as I make you come again and again and again."

Just that quickly she was trembling, arousal coating her sex and heating her thighs. He inhaled. "Makers, you smell amazing. I don't think I can wait to taste you." He knelt in front of her and she gasped, grabbing his shoulders as he pressed an open-mouthed kiss against her clit. He spread the lips of her pussy wide and flattened his tongue against her, as if he were absorbing her into his blood stream.

Z growled against her sex, the vibration weakening her knees until she was leaning heavily against him, her body bowing over his, hair grazing his back. He grabbed her waist, pulling her down to the floor and lifting her legs over his shoulders.

Dorothy lifted her head to watch him staring at her from between her thighs. She felt a moment's insecurity. Her body was totally visible, completely open to him. He sensed her hesitation. “You have the most sensual body I’ve ever seen. Soft curves of silk and cream. I could drown in you. You are a goddess, sweet Dorothy. Let me worship you.”

Her head fell back against the cool floor as he disappeared between her legs. She gasped when his tongue thrust deep inside her sex, his palms spreading her ass cheeks wide, opening her completely to him.

When his thumb, damp with her juices, pressed against her ass, she trembled. Hadn’t she fantasized, as she’d watched him entering that young, beautiful man, watching the look of pain and ecstasy on his angelic face as the wizard rode him that first night? Hadn’t she touched herself and dreamt of him inside her in that way? So forbidden. So wanton. Oh God.

He pushed through the tight muscles, biting her inner thigh at her groan. “No one has ever touched you here.” It wasn’t a question. “I will. I want you on your knees, begging for my cock in your ass. Shit, I could come just thinking about how you’ll feel around me. You’re so tight, baby, but you can take me.” He twisted his thumb inside her, and she screamed at the fullness.

“Not yet, but soon. Now I want to feel you come against my tongue, taste your sweet cream.” His actions matched his words, his tongue sliding deep inside her pussy, fucking her as he pushed his thumb in and out of her ass.